SAVAGES

By

Christina Bergling

HellBound Books Publishing LLC

A HellBound Books LLC Publication

www.hellboundbookspublishing.com

Printed in the United States of America

Also by Christina Bergling from
HellBound Books Publishing LLC

The Waning

Savages

Christina Bergling

SAVAGES

Savages

1

We sat in the middle of the field, he and I, feeling like the last man and woman on Earth.

Wind swept the tall grass, making the bloodstained blades dance. They bowed to the song of the breeze while the blood dripped from them red and slow. The sun poured down quietly on this otherwise calm and clear day. We just breathed, both sitting among the grass and amidst the carnage, arms propped on our knees, weapons still dangling from limp fingertips. The wind spirited the sounds of our respiration away, snatching the air from our lungs and sucking it far across the quiet world.

I stared out ahead of me, past the field and down into the empty town—what remained of another small American city, with what was left of the populace in pieces at our feet. How long would I smell like them this time? How long would we haunt their abandoned houses and scavenge their stagnant grocery stores?

This view could have been on a post card. The town probably used pictures shot from this very point for their tourism website. The lush field sprawled down until it washed up against the quaint buildings, hills rolling out to the sides. The sun's rays split the few clouds, casting light and gentle shadows. Without the severed limbs and mangled torsos in the foreground, it was quite picturesque.

I looked down.

A finger lay curled around the toe of my shoe. It reached up through the grass as if coming out of the ground itself. Yet it stretched out in isolation. There was no hand, no body—just a lonely, marred finger left behind. At one point I would have recoiled, shrunk away from death this close to me. I would have personalized this finger, imagining the memories in the flesh and the life it led. It would have been a piece of a human being, and that would have stirred the empathetic humanity in me. I just sat there, looking and breathing, noting the line of dirt crusted deep under the fingernail. It was just another dead body part.

I finally nudged it with my foot, letting the digit rest haphazardly in the dirt, like the rest of the pieces peeking out of the grass like twisted lawn gnomes.

The sound of the blood was near deafening over the gentle wind. It was simply everywhere, falling from the grass, from the pieces; dribbling lazily, dragging out each drop, making itself known. I couldn't help but think about the chocolate blood I had made for Halloween costumes, how much it looked just like the real thing now all around me. My mouth almost involuntarily watered, remembering that forgotten taste of chocolate.

An empty eye found me from between wilted blades, staring out from a skull cleaved in half, awkwardly fixed on me without seeing me—without seeing *anything* ever again. I could tell that the eye was blue, but they all looked milky without life behind them. The more I saw these dead eyes every day, the less they looked like people. They could have been slabs of meat at a butcher shop, they could have been road kill on the shoulder of the highway. It was all the same now.

Beside me, he looked past all this, past the crimson field, the fingers and legs, past the vacant eyes. He stared out ahead, above our sad little reality—like he was always able to do. Leaving me behind, grounded in my discontented flesh.

As the sun meandered across the sky and the moments stretched out long across us, I grew restless wallowing in our aftermath. I began to fidget. I shifted my weight from hip to hip, moved my legs in, then stretched them back out. I looked at him, back at the town, down at the victims. My breathing tightened as I waited on him.

He just existed in his space, sitting like a statue beside me. His arms rested apathetically against his knees as the mingling of blood and dirt stained the bottoms of his pant legs. The colors grew and crept upward, invading the fabric further with each passing day, each battle. His sword hung permanently from his curled fingers, continuing to let wayward droplets of blood splash to the grass.

Ballistic sunglasses perpetually obscured his eyes, but I could tell his gaze ventured out past our horizon. What I truly knew of his face was a sharp nose bearing the leathered abuse of so many days traveling under the sun and thin lips that never turned up. His mouth only moved to instruct or antagonize me. He managed constantly to battle back the hair sprouting from his head, keeping it close and clean. Everything always in order.

To him, this was just another place; these were just more neutralized threats. It all just *was*. It did not change him. He let it break over him like waves against the rocky beach. And I envied him. I could never escape. I could never flee the moment. My only alternative was to tumble into the past, which was far more dangerous.

Then without a word, he stood, and I followed. He led me down the field and toward the town, stepping over the dismembered bodies without looking down at them. I let my eyes swing from side to side, sweeping the leftovers. Seven, by my best fast count. It was easiest to count the heads, or what was left of them. Limbs just got too confusing, four on each body, carved into however many pieces, strewn far and wide. Heads were larger, easier to spot and easier to count.

There was the milky-eyed half head that had been staring at me, a skull blown open out the back with its body sprawled down the hill, an ear with hair poking out among the blades, a bloody rock on top of what I remembered was a head, three other round lumps protruding from the grass. Seven heads. Even less than the last town.

Where were they going? Were they killing each other off, like they tried to do to us? Were they just dying off?

The field spilled into the streets of the small and quiet town. He led me down the empty road lined on both sides with abandoned cars. A minivan had half mounted the curb when it collided with a parking meter. The side windows were smashed out, and I thought I saw blood on the leftover frame. I could hear the echoes of screams as the passengers were dragged out. A luxury sedan was parked with the doors gaping open. A briefcase and umbrella tumbled out onto the concrete, worthless now.

All the towns looked the same. I wasn't even sure what state we were in anymore, those boundaries no longer existed. It didn't matter where we fell on the map, it was all the same. Nothing moved in these forsaken places. There were no sounds, as if all of the animals had fled as well. It was eerie, stagnant, unsettling. Something in my survival instincts could not sit in the dead silence. Yet I always looked for something: another maniacal survivor, a dog, a bird. I cast my eyes down forgotten alleyways and over relics of lives left behind.

The side street we entered converged with downtown. Tall buildings narrowed the sky, split the ground before us into stripes of shadow. He walked two or three steps ahead of me and to the side— enough to keep me in his peripherals. I caught his head shift slightly in my direction, making sure I was still in my place, still calm and following. His wind- burned cheek betrayed the wrinkles that grew deeper by the day.

I imagined him before, in the previous life: close-shaven in desert camo BDUs, doing whatever it was soldiers did when they weren't at war. I had known nothing personally about the military or soldiers in the past life. Only a jumble of stereotypes dancing in my head. Empty crew cut heads bobbing on top of combat boots and marching into gun shops, strip clubs, and tattoo parlors. Not people so much as a faceless collective. I never wanted to *know*, I wanted to stay safely separate and civilian. Yet now this faded soldier I followed was all that remained.

We both clutched our weapons close for comfort, kept our limbs tucked in tight, our hackles up. Lessons painfully learned. What was dubbed just a sweeping shadow was revealed as the long knife that nearly sank into my shoulder. What was dismissed as a gust of wind had been the first of a flailing pack of wild-eyed savages cornering us in an alley. Everything was a threat.

As we trudged, my mind strayed dangerously from the risk mitigation at hand, from analyzing every inch and every flutter, and took gentle and seemingly innocent side steps into questions. Moving through all

11

that was, the empty buildings and the dead streets, I wondered what I always wondered when we were in a town. Out on the road, it was easy to forget civilization had even existed before it all utterly fucking collapsed. However, here in the remnants, I always heard the question echoing around inside me: had the world ended everywhere else? Were they drinking wine in Paris, playing soccer in England, flying a plane in China, reading and watching on the news how America had collapsed, how the government had imploded, how there was no country left and its people were scavenging off each other?

I could imagine them all carrying on with their normal lives, all we lost just a colorful story on the screen or the page. Laughing at how all those fat, lazy, dumb Americans got what they deserved. How it was always inevitable. I would hate and resent them if I could fully believe they were out there living like we once did.

The scraping of his boots on the street halted and brought me back to the fallout of our reality. I stopped behind him two or three steps back and to the side. Instinctually and habitually, I pivoted to face the opposite direction, turning my back to him, watching our backs and tracing our trail for followers.

"Grocery ahead on the left," he said.

"Do you really think anything is left? If they survived this long, they had to have raided it," I replied.

"Worth a check. Unless you have somewhere to be."

I laughed softly to myself as we fell back in step. Carts stood at random, alone among the few cars in the parking lot. Another scene of suspended animation. Any appearance of normalcy or order was unnerving. Cars no longer belonged parked between lines of paint on the asphalt, shopping carts no longer needed to be racked up for collection. I didn't like to remember how things used to be. I would rather traverse an empty, barren crater than amble through relics and reminders.

There were two rotting bodies on the pavement, long decayed from their fleshy start. One skeleton lay twisted and reaching alone in the center of the pool of black asphalt, frozen in his dying disappointment. Another was contorted and collapsed into a pile of sticky bones on a median that probably used to have plush grass. Those horrors were the new normal; dead bodies did not make me cringe nearly as much as a place setting left abandoned on a dinner table.

"They didn't bury their dead," I mused, stepping over the sprawling failure on our way across. Wrinkled bills waved in one gnarled hand, now completely and utterly useless. It wouldn't even make good kindling. Once they killed you and left your money, it was all truly over.

"Less human the farther we get."

"Then why do we keep going in this direction?"

"We're running out of directions to go. You've seen what happens if we stay."

They came breaking through the walls of an abandoned apartment complex, they came pouring through the halls like water. Eventually, they heard us. Eventually, they found us.

I nodded reluctantly.

The doors to the store were long since broken out and ripped away, the floor covered in months of dirt and leaves blown in from a world gradually reclaiming the building. Daylight poured in from the front before dissipating among the aisles. It was as I expected. Ransacked, picked over, stripped down to the bare, stinking bones.

I could smell the rot from the produce section, from what had turned before the looters came, the stench of thawed and decayed flesh from the deli section. No one

13

believed it was the end until it was too late, until what was left had already started to spoil.

We separated at the center and fanned out in opposite directions, both walking to the farthest aisle to scout, and weaved our way back together. I gripped my cutlass tightly, blade hovering up at the ready. The handle belonged in my hand, the steel an extension of my body. This inanimate object that traveled everywhere with me since plucking it from yet another festering corpse, that kept me company in these endless wandering miles, that he taught me to use as a survival tool. My fingers had worn grooves in the wood of the handle, branding it as only mine.

The shelves stood largely raided, only tattered remnants and a few stragglers crouched in the darkness. I snagged a can of peaches from under the shelves in the canned fruit aisle. I found a couple dented cans of dog food. A lone bag of chips huddled discarded near the putrid fruit, still closed. We converged in the feminine hygiene aisle, where I slipped a crushed box of generic tampons in my bag.

"Anything?" he asked.

"Couple cans. Mostly dog food. You?"

"Nothing really. Everything left is rotten. There were some diapers and formula but not much."

"Yeah, the kids died first. Formula could make emergency food though."

"I'll grab it just in case. You don't need diapers, do you?"

"Nope, already handled. Potty trained for some time now."

I listened to his footsteps and mentally traced him back to the baby aisle while I waited near the front. As a child, I loved being in empty places. There was something special and sneaky about being in a normally busy place when it was closed, dark, vacant. It made it feel like it belonged to me, my own private session with something public. I remembered feeling at peace walking down the hall of my childhood church after hours or alone in the diner I worked at before it opened. Now the whole world was an abandoned shell, and it didn't feel like anything belonged to me. It felt like they all forgot me when they went. I would have given anything for one bustling grocery store, one disgruntled shopper complaining as he rushed home with groceries for his family, one apathetic store cashier texting her way through her shift.

"I'm sure formula will make a delicious dinner," he said, walking back up to me.

We moved back into the light from the door and sat on the floor, leaned up against the counter for one of the registers. He pulled out his canteen and took a long swig from it before passing it to me. I held up the bag of chips. A score like this could not wait.

"Chips?" he looked astonished. "Unopened?" I nodded.

He tore into the bag and lifted one chip out gently. He placed it on his tongue and crunched it slowly, closing his eyes.

"I never did care for barbecue chips," he said. He paused, chewing slowly again. "Best chip I've ever had."

We passed the food and drink between the two of us in our post-slaughter ritual. Breaking bread after battle. The throbbing of fight faded from my cells, the flashing blur of blood and limbs and twisted faces stopped flickering in front of my eyes. It slipped out of our present and started to file itself among the now far too many memories.

He fell stoic again, letting his hand massage his ragged chin as his gaze wandered out from the store and away from me. His eyes dropped deep as his focus stretched out past us. His muscles settled as he let his mind loose. Wherever he went, wherever he found refuge.

I closed my eyes, breathed, and savored a chip. I remembered chowing down on so many potato chips in my measly college dorm room until my jeans grew tighter by the day. I remembered how it seemed right to eat whatever the hell I wanted at last, stop sleeping, and start drinking until my liver wanted to resign. Each time the salty goodness crunched and echoed against my teeth, I saw a flash of the Christmas lights I had taped to my standard issue furniture.

Almost as if he could hear my wayward thoughts, he snapped to attention and stood, dusting off his filthy clothes.

"Let's hit the houses, find somewhere to hold up for the night at least."

He took his place two to three steps ahead of me and to the side, and we marched out of the store.

2

We wandered farther down the same street, pressing on past the office buildings with shattered high windows and puddles of decomposed jumpers melted on the sidewalk; past the convenient fast food chains with burned out cars piled up in their drive-thrus, past the parks where the grass and trees had been put to flame and had left the playground equipment standing like charred skeletons.

We transitioned into a neighborhood. Cookie-cutter houses distinguished only by which were riddled with bullet holes or had the windows blown out or were scorched by fire. A few always managed to sneak past untouched, some kind of random salvation in chaos. I saw the first as he did. His steps turned to guide us toward a brown house. Its fence had collapsed around the backyard, but the windows remained intact, boarded up.

They had obviously lived here.

"This one," he gestured. "Another adjoining the backyard."

"They looked decently fed," I said. "Might have a stockpile in one of the houses."

I watched the back of his head nod and felt a little sick to my stomach that I could so nonchalantly evaluate our attackers to gauge what we might pillage from their camps. So many starving nights made it easy. So many grizzled expressions as they tried to kill us made it easy. The others seemed less and less like people each time. It was us and them, and they were tantamount to animals snarling at our throats.

He wouldn't consider eating them. Even in the darkest depths of our hunger, he said it was beneath us, almost as if they weren't worthy of our consumption. It had crossed my mind, as my stomach climbed aching in between my jaws, as every cell of my body throbbed and begged for any morsel. He had held me as I howled wildly and simply whispered to me, "We are better than this. We will find something."

And we did. He always found something for us. A day later with a roasted squirrel in my gut, I felt only shame at pleading to eat a man who had ambushed us with an axe. I couldn't look into his eyes for another two days.

"Front door?" he said, a statement and a question.

I broke from his path and climbed the small stairs to the cement porch of the house. Pieces of the fallen fence hung sloppily nailed over the large window beside the door. Thrown up hastily and askew, their nails bent and slammed in sideways. Hatch marks peppered the wood and siding from an attack, where someone had tried to force their way in.

Crushed against the bottom of the house, buried under dust out of sight, I could make out the remains of a doll and a toy car. A plastic leg jutted up from the dirt beside clumps of matted synthetic hair. The rest of the doll was impacted in the ground, half buried like a tiny corpse. I could not make out the color of the toy car. All brown, I could discern the small wheels, the recognizable shape. I felt my knees swoon as a flash of my son on the carpet with his fleet of toy cars threatened to wash up over me. He duplicated the rumbling noises of motors and the squealing of tires as he smashed the small toys together. He turned his face up to me as he smiled when he realized I laughed as I watched him. I snapped back to this reality, to the dusty broken toys of dead children, by the sound of his footsteps on the roof.

I could track his movements on the house by the sound—the *only* sound in the silence. I could picture him entering and moving through the house in his standard, practiced execution. Always through the roof. It puzzled me as to how they never thought to fortify the attic or roof and how they never thought to attack through the roof. They were all open and vulnerable, easy.

I followed the sound of his boots across the shingles, slow and methodical. They scuffed from where he scaled the wall, making a small perimeter then settling at the distant edge. Next, I heard the splintering smash, which I assumed to be the small vent into the attic. Pieces tumbled down to softly thud on the dead grass as he cleared his entry. Bumps and fumbling through the confined space; I could almost taste the stale air with him. I closed my eyes to put my mind with him and avoid those damned toys.

I heard the attic ladder slam down followed by a quick series of footsteps weaving their way closer to me. There was a scrape on the other side of the door as he lifted the bar bracing it, the rub of metal as he slid the latch, the click as he twisted the locks. Then he held the door open for me.

I stepped in cautiously, almost crouching into the dim light. It was a house, once even a home. The comforts of carpet and stairs and walls seemed more foreign the longer we were on the road. Shelter seemed instinctually confining. I felt my body shrink into itself, tight and guarded in what used to define my normal.

The furniture was largely gone. I imagine they burned it through the winter. The empty rooms reminded me of house hunting with my husband with a bump on my belly. Walking into these strange and empty houses and concocting futures out of them, him holding my hand by the ends of my fingers as he led me through each one. I tried to fight all these artifacts of life that threatened to rip me into memory and regret. Ghosts and phantoms were licking at my neck as I pushed through the now vacant house.

We went to the kitchen first. Food always took priority. He turned on the faucet, and it sputtered a bit of black water into the sink before he shut it back off.

"Unfortunate," I said. "You think they found ground water?"

He grunted and turned to the fridge. As he took the handle in one hand, he lifted his small knife in the other. I pressed my back into the counter and rested my fingers on my cutlass. We both took a breath together, and he snatched the door open.

Empty, dark, surprisingly clean. He rolled his eyes and let the door fall closed.

I shrugged. Empty was better than a rabid raccoon, or a stack of severed hands, or the wrapped corpse of a newborn as we had found in other refrigerators. I let my hand fall on the knob of the cabinet. I noticed the white handle with small pink flowers brushed on it looked exactly like those in my grandmother's kitchen, where I would climb into the pots cabinet and eat crackers in my cave.

Damn this house.

Was I really even here? Was this just another starving fever dream in the desert? I slipped my hand into my pocket and pinched my thigh until my hand trembled. Pain blazed up my nerves and flashed over my body. Nope, not dreaming.

My grandmother's weathered pots and pans did not greet me in the cabinet.

"Holy shit," I said, mouth agape.

He stopped opening and slamming empty drawers and turned. I held the cabinet doors open and turned to him, my jaw still dangling.

"Holy shit," he breathed.

From top to bottom, the cabinet was stacked with canned goods. Rows and rows of glorious pictures of baked beans, corn, fruit cocktail, cocktail weenies, Spam. My stomach seized as the well-composed pictures got my mouth watering. This could feed us for weeks, months. I could almost feel myself smiling.

"Preppers?" I laughed.

"Close enough. Love those crazy bastards!" He took a can of beans in his hand and gave it an almost affectionate, longing look. "We need a bag or something to tote this shit around."

"We can't stay?"

"Only a night or two. You know the drill. Can't risk them having scouts or parties coming back home, or those other drifters."

"Always have to keep moving."

"Right."

I was so tired of moving. Even faced with this upsetting house, the thought of continuing to trudge out on the road crushed down on my mind.

He walked out of the kitchen a little lighter. I would venture to say almost skipping through the shadows if I didn't know him better. I trailed behind him, letting a smile tease at my lips. Food. One major necessity handled in the immediate, allowing us, for just the briefest of seconds, to think about anything else.

"Bug out bags!" I heard him yell from one of the back rooms. "Ditch that rejected high school shit - we finally got you a proper bag."

There were four of them propped in the corner, straps facing out, ready to go.

"Why didn't they bug out?" I asked as he pushed one into my arms. I dropped with the weight of it.

"Too scared maybe. Thought they could secure things here better. They did for a while, clearly."

"Until we came along."

"Until they came after us."

He was like a kid at Christmas, tearing open the bag and marveling over its contents. He sat on the floor and pulled the first bag between his legs, letting his twitching feet betray his composure. I stood behind him and leaned against the wall, like I had many times over the shoulders of my boys attacking their latest present or toy.

Once he was settled, he slowly unzipped the bag and spread it open. He began plunging his hands in and meticulously lining up the contents on the carpet beside him.

Three plastic bottles and several sheets of tablets. "Water filtration bottles and iodine tablets," he said.

Thin silver packages with labels on the front. "Dehydrated food."

A small folded square of silver fabric. "Reflective mat."

A crushed box of Ziploc bags, a bag with matches lining the bottom, another with a crushed roll of toilet paper. "Dry bags."

A small axe with a leather sheath, a black hunting knife in a canvas holster, a folded camping shovel, a couple of small black boxes. "Tools, obviously. Compass. Flint."

A spool of wire with a hook stuck into the top. "Fishing gear."

At the bottom, a couple of bundles. "Tent, blankets, a couple long sleeved shirts."

"Holy shit," I said again.

"You can say that again. And again."

I could not deny that this one house was a lifesaver. We could survive off these scores for months, longer. It was an unfamiliar idea. I did not quite know how to process it, how to accept the concept that we could be okay for just a moment.

"Bring me some of that food," he said. "We're going to need to repack these bags, take as much as we can."

"What do we do with what we can't take?"

"Not sure. I don't want to leave any of it. We'll probably never be back here again. But it would be such a waste. Let me see what we can fit first."

I returned to the kitchen that had gone from haunting to salvation and began stacking the cans of goods into my arms. My cutlass felt foreign and abandoned dangling from my belt, bouncing against my leg. It belonged in my hand, it lived in my fingers. I took a breath and lowered it down, let it hang lifeless for the moment. Food was always the priority. I almost wanted to let myself enjoy the moment and the sweet sensation of all the weight and cans pressing into my forearms.

I walked awkwardly back down the hall, leaning back to allow the cans to balance on my chest. One, then two, leapt from my arms and bounced off my foot and against the carpet. I should have flinched at the noise, at identifying our position. Yet I just smiled to myself and continued my mission.

I knelt next to him and piled the cans beside his itemized array of new supplies. Then I turned to retrieve the fallen cans and their other compatriots.

"There's no way it all fits," I said over his shoulder when the entire mound was next to him.

"Have a little faith. Food is the priority - obviously, but canned goods are heavy. We can sacrifice some of this other shit; we've been living without it long enough. But we take as much food as we can bear to carry."

He propped two empty bags up beside him and began lining the bottoms with cans. After each layer, he hefted the bags to test the weight. Then he continued stacking. Once the bags dragged hard toward the ground when he lifted them, he began to fill in the space with the meager possessions from our former bags and the supplies from the floor.

A small pile of cans did remain on the floor, but I was impressed at how much he had managed to Tetris into those bug out bags.

Calmly, I looked down at him. Then the wave swelled up within me, taking me by surprise and causing me to waver in my boots. Every cell in my body screamed out to touch him. Repopulate. Flesh. Connection. Yet every iota of my logic screamed *no*. Somewhere within me, primal wiring crossed, carnage intersected carnal, adrenaline begged endorphins. After being so close to death, I wanted to feel alive. With each survival, I felt closer to him, and something in me begged to consummate that.

My desire for him was like my desire to eat my gun every morning. It was not something I did - it was something I lived with.

"We gotta check the other house," he said, thankfully snapping me back to myself.

The finds had animated him, he was no longer trudging. He had been infected by an energy different than that of victory. I strained to separate my consciousness as far as possible from my foolish flesh and focused on following him again. We abandoned our former bags on the dingy, flattened carpet and heaved their replacements onto our backs.

We exited through the sliding glass door into the backyard, which adjoined three others. The deck furniture twisted into a barely recognizable mass of metal and shattered glass. The grass had long ago perished, and it crunched under our feet. A doghouse slumped forgotten beside the fallen fence.

That's when we heard it, the sound piercing the silent world. It split my skull. My uterus tightened, and my nipples flushed as if milk was flooding in. It was the cry of a child, that unmistakable infant scream.

3

He froze in front of me, mid-stride, one foot dangling above the ground. When was the last time we had heard a child? Could children still exist in this place? Something familiar and forgotten welled up inside me. Quivering, my breathing fall quick and shallow, and tears fell on my cheeks.

The world started to flicker as I hyperventilated. He turned and tipped his ballistic sunglasses forward to look at me before the scene blinked out. In these endless seconds, I saw the square lights of the delivery room, the blonde curls tied back on the nurse coaching me and holding my anesthetized leg, the blue cap of the doctor looking between my legs. *Dante's hand clutched my shoulder as he leaned forward anxiously. I was losing him to the moment, to his anticipation. My lungs were burning as Goldilocks counted eight...nine...ten... beside me. My leg trembled in her arms; my face contorted as I pushed, pushed blindly into relief. "It's a boy," Dante was crying. I felt a smile tease my exhausted lips. Then his cry ruptured the world.*

I threw up the barbecue chips at our feet.

We didn't speak. He continued to look at me over dusty sunglasses, volumes spoken in that silence. For the first time in our many months or years, I thought I might have seen fear in the edges of his face, actual panic; somewhere writhing beneath well-checking me. This was something he did not know how to handle.

The continued sound of the infant shrieking brought me back. I breathed deliberately through my mouth as I followed him, counting my exhales like in yoga to focus my mind, keeping those hazardous memories at bay.

Eight...nine...ten...

The sound persisted, kept shooting out of the next house at us like arrows, threatening to fracture the planet until it divided underneath us and swallowed us whole. How could a sound that once governed my world be so foreign and unbelievable? I didn't know I could want to die more than I did the day before, *any* of those hellish days before. It was as if I could feel the sound breaking against me, as if we were battling our way against prevailing winds.

We marched tentatively across the brittle grass and into the house that shared the backyard. Their small community. No safety procedures this time. No cautious casing and entry. He plowed through the sliding glass door, barreled through the kitchen without a glance to evaluate any resources. The child lured him in with singular focus.

The interior of the house whipped past me in a blur as I kept my eyes to his back and my steps at his heels. My heart thudded in my ears as I just kept counting my breath and following mechanically.

We found him in a closet at the top of the stairs. A closet - smart, more secure. His small body was swaddled in tattered blankets on the floor. He could be left on the floor alone while his parents went to slay

27

drifters, since he was too young to move. He was conceived and born into this disgusting world; he would have no memory of the one we mourned that had come before it.

He stopped in front of the closet, frozen, arms down at his sides, weapons still in hand. He just stared down at the whimpering ball of flesh. Then, suddenly, he roused. Snapping back into himself, he slipped his sword into its sheath on his back, tucked his gun into a holster, and bent down very slowly as he reached to cradle the infant.

I couldn't watch. The hallway closed in around me. It was suddenly so stifling, so unsafe. The sound of my own erratic breathing deafened me. My hands went numb and I could feel myself starting to shake. I turned and ran. I sprinted down the carpeted steps, over the torn linoleum in the kitchen, back out into the glaring light of the dead backyard. My steps were sloppy and desperate. I staggered out onto the rotten grass and just meandered in a circle, digging my hands into my hair.

He had the small child enveloped in his arms when he caught up to me, ratty blanket dangling out from his embrace. He was looking down at the child, whose fit had now dwindled to shuddering sobs. The baby was bright red from screaming. I turned away from them and leaned forward with my hands on my knees, struggling to find my breath. He stepped around me to face me and just looked up at me calmly.

"If we take this child, it will get us killed," I finally said.

"If we don't, what we have done will kill this child."

"Children die now. They all die. This world is not good enough for them anymore. I had children. I buried my babies."

"You're a mother, and you can say that?"

"I say that because I am a mother. *Was* a mother. I miss my babies every day, but I would rather them be buried than living through this."

"We killed his chance. We did that. Not this world. He's our responsibility."

"Is that like intervening when a woman is being beaten to death? It would be a mercy not a tragedy."

"Was it mercy in that field today?"

"No. That was survival. The survival you taught me."

"So what then? We leave him to starve? We beat his head in with a rock like the fucking savages? Tell me."

I had no words. I stood breathing, reeling. As always, I could not argue with him, no matter how my very core screamed against it. I could not walk his line unless he dragged me.

"You expect me to be his new mother," I said coldly, looking away.

"I expect you to be a human being. We are still that after all—humans. As long as we're living."

"One happy family," I muttered, turning and storming back into the second house.

A baby. How could there be a baby in this world? How could he want to take this baby around this world? This was going to get us fucking killed. I could not be around that goddamn baby, could not have it stirring up all I buried in those two small graves. I felt the throbbing of rage and panic and fear and pain and every single heavy emotion that had ever slammed through my veins. My eyes were welling up, and I was teetering on the edge of the present again.

"This one looks like me, too," Dante cooed into my ear as the new babe suckled at my breast between us. Dante pressed his hand against the top of the tiny head as I ran my finger slowly along the miniature arm. "No baby, not so lucky this time," I replied calmly. "Those are my eyes. Just you wait."

29

I crouched against a wall sobbing as my former life receded.

Dante. Jordi. Eli.

I could not keep their names from dancing in the wrinkles of my brain. Three sets of eyes, two brown and one hazel, staring at me, dead and lifeless. Three voices echoed around my mind, beckoning me from the past. I could not escape my boys; their ghosts perpetually possessed me, held me permanently as their prisoner to our lost and haunted life. They pulled me into the undertow, a sea of memory nearly drowned me then abandoned me once more. They left me sputtering on the empty shore.

Alone.

I knew I was softly crying, though it didn't matter. A day had not gone by without tears gracing my cheeks since the first of the horrors started washing up on our life. My eyes and face were anesthetized, immune. As if what I felt mattered anymore.

The counting returned, the slow breathing. My mind lapped back up on the shore of the real. I could feel the present reality by the suicidal drone humming in my bones. I mopped up my face on my sleeve and pulled my shit together.

We would need supplies.

4

Breathe. One…two…three…

I grounded myself back on that matted carpet, reinforced the tangibility of the walls around me, tethered myself to the reality of the moment. I slowly crept up the wall, pressing my back hard as I inched to standing. I let my fingertips trail the drywall, reading the horrors in the Braille of its texture.

I would trudge forward; I would follow his lead—as always.

With a kitchen like theirs, I knew these quasi preppers were organized. But did they turn before the new addition? Did they care for this child as the humans they were or the animals we dismembered? I took small baby steps toward his swaddling closet, then stood staring into it.

Four…five…six…seven…

The closet was dark. I had to lean down to peer at the empty shelves. Another couple of blankets lay crumpled in the back of the floor. I clawed them out and slung them over my shoulder. Nothing else. I turned to explore the bedrooms we had yet to case.

I imagined the mother, whichever body pieces she happened to be, had been breastfeeding him. I could not see a filthy, growling savage leaned over a camp stove, warming up formula. But I couldn't see any of these savages, or whatever they were, caring for an infant. They hadn't eaten him, and that was something.

The stench of the first room nearly knocked me backward out of the doorframe. In a blur of watery vision, I saw the shit smeared on the walls from the adjoining bathroom, filth gradually taking over the house. I stumbled back, coughing and heaving, wondering why in the fuck they didn't just shit and piss outside.

Eight…nine…ten…

Fuck this stupid excuse for a world. One more bedroom. I could do this.

I walked more cautiously still, leaning back to guard my nose. I pressed one finger against my nostrils, hoping the smell of my own dirty flesh would wash out the particles. The door creaked softly as I swung it open.

No stench. No shit. Thank God.

The light broke through the mangled blinds still clinging to the one window. Twisted shadows carved up the blank walls. A couple of mattresses lay heaped and soiled in the corner. I let my fingers find the handle of my cutlass as I eased in toward the closet. The doors hung crooked off their tracks. Dirty handprints decorated the edges. Different sizes, different shapes, smears. Finger paintings on my own stainless steel fridge, dangling by strawberry magnets, flashed through my mind. As I shook the image loose, my hand flinched on my weapon.

One…two…three…

I stepped forward and put my head into the closet. The floor was piled with the skeletons of metal hangers. A couple of baseball bats and large sticks stood in one corner. And that was it—fucking nothing. For all their preparation for the end of the world, they sure as hell weren't prepared for anything now. Definitely not for him.

Neither were we.

I let a breath escape my lips as I pressed my hand to the wall outside the closet before retreating.

I found him standing in the center of the communal yard still cradling the infant. His back was to me as he swayed side to side, looking down at the now sleeping bundle. From the back of my brain, I heard Dante's low voice spilling out of the nursery. *"Rock-a-bye... And goodnight..."*

I had never seen him distracted, never seen him with his guard down. I could run up behind him and put my cutlass through his throat before he had time to drop the baby. I didn't know what he looked like with his eyes not scanning and processing. They were locked on that child, a familiar silhouette framed only by fallout and destruction.

I lingered in the doorframe hesitantly with my nails picking at the vinyl. Then I took one more breath before I dropped down from the house onto the stiff grass and announced my return.

"Nothing," I said as I walked toward him.

I couldn't look him in the eye. I couldn't take him with that child.

"They were gone by the time he came then," he replied.

"Yeah, so it would seem."

"We'll have to raid the store again. Lucky we snagged that formula."

"Lucky we found food for us."

"We'll hit another store. On our way out of town."

"Are we leaving tonight?"

"For the best, I think. Don't want to risk there being any others nearby."

"Because he's going to make noise?"

"Yes."

"Where are we headed?"

"West, still."

"Westward, ho." I turned to start walking back through the first house. "I'm not carrying it."

And I kept walking. I grabbed one of the bug out bags and fled the joined prepper-houses-gone-wild. I chased our path out of that ghostly suburbia, and I heard his footsteps falling in step behind me.

My heart pounded in my ears, the entire world throbbed. My vision began to blur deeper around the edges. I could almost *see* the sound of my banging pulse. Colors became more vivid, the light brighter. My senses pricked on painful edge. I locked my head forward, refused even to turn enough to grant the child my peripherals, yet my mind's eye was staring at it. My brain was utterly fixated on the tiny body.

I pursed my lips tightly and forced my breath out hard between them. I knew he could hear the erratic sound, but it was the only thing keeping me in my skin at that moment—my skin that was ablaze, my flesh that felt foreign and confining, my mind that was twisting inward against me.

Deep in my chest, somewhere that used to swell at the sight of my babies, I felt a rotting ache. At my core, my arms begged to comfort the infant, to remember what it felt like to nurture. Yet even the acknowledgement of that instinct had my chest closing and nausea bubbling up along my throat.

I choked it back. I wanted to tear my pack off and rip at my own hair. I wanted to scream and slam my fists against his face. I wanted to curl into a ball and cry hysterically.

I just kept walking. Marching on. One step in front of the other. West. For no fucking reason.

"What should we call him?" he said from behind me. He had waited until my breathing fell calm again.

"No."

"We can't call a baby *no*."

"We do not name this child. Not when he's not ours. Not when we killed his parents, his people. Not when he doesn't have a chance in hell of surviving."

"Not naming the puppy, eh? He's a person, and people have names. I'll call him Xavier."

"Why Xavier?"

"Strong name. Smart, professor-like even."

"You're not talking fucking X-Men. You want to name the child after a comic book mutant?"

"Yeah. It's a legit name. Huh, little Xavier?"

That almost made me smile. Almost. I dropped the anger from my step and allowed him to catch up to me. I still couldn't look at him as we walked side by side. I kept my cutlass in a tight grip since his hands were occupied. We stepped in silence as the blocks slipped past. My mind raced ahead.

"Do you think they were just like us?" I finally said. "Do you think they were surviving here and we came through and threatened it? Do you think we were their savages?"

"No," he said with finality. "You saw them on that hill."

"And I saw that fucking house."

"What was in the house?"

"A lot of shit." I paused. "No, I *literally* mean shit. God, it was smeared everywhere."

"Yeah, they were animals."

"Do you think he'll be the same as them?"

"No," he replied again. "Babies are innocent."

"Spoken like someone who never raised a toddler." I almost laughed. "We are born little savages to our core. Biting, screaming, stealing savages. Civilization is practically beaten into us, our parents spent the better part of a decade getting us there."

"Xavier is not them. I wouldn't let him be them."

I wanted to say we wouldn't survive long enough to see, but I didn't have that fight in me today. I felt drained and lifeless now, shambling like a zombie through this apocalypse.

By the time we left the second store, I had found my way to my place behind him again. The miraculous score of a baby carrier liberated his arms. In all our pillaging, I had never noticed that so much baby and children's supplies had survived because the children had not. He strode on with his head up, aware again and weapons in hand. The child, sated with a cold bottle of formula, snoozed against him.

The town ebbed into our past along with the remnants of civilization. We broke back out onto a patch of undeveloped country. It would be easier to forget the world that was and the traces that remained of it—it always was—until the next haunted ruins, the next empty city. He led us into the sunset like a cliché until we were surrounded by only the world. Then, by the light of dusk, he made us camp.

I watched him awkwardly fumble with the infant on his chest. He attempted to tip sideways to collect wood off the ground, angling and leaning to keep the tiny head in place. He tried to step his feet far apart to lower himself and stabilize his movements. The baby did not cooperate, of course. He thrust his unstable head in the opposite direction, whimpered and whined at every effort. I wanted to see him frustrated, I wanted him to pay for this decision.

I did my part, gathering wood and wrenching open one of our new cans of food, but I would not relieve him of that child. I kept him in the corner of my eye simply to observe his faltering. His inexperience showed and almost made me smile. Almost. It reminded me too much of my own dead husband blundering as a new father. I could see Dante taking a newborn in his arms for the first time under the strange fluorescent lights of the hospital room, juggling the head and the body in a sloppy attempt to keep both supported. *The baby made the muted newborn cry as his little fists flailed in the air. Dante bit his lip as he both smiled and frowned. "I got you, little man," he said to the child. "I'll figure this out."*

By the time it was dark, I could hear the gentle snore of the child in his lap over the soft popping of the fire. He and I both separately tumbled in and out of entranced thoughts as we finished eating. Physically beside each other, mentally worlds apart.

"Did I ever tell you about my wife?" he said.

I stopped chewing. For a second, the fire just crackled between us as I sat stunned, slack-jawed, and silent. What he had told me, that first night after rescuing me in a bloody heap, was, *"We have no pasts. Those lives and those loves are as dead as these things here. Don't ask about mine. Don't tell me about yours."*

I snapped out of my startle, reanimated my lips. "No."

He stopped for a moment, staring quietly in the fire, before sucking in a breath and kind of smiling.

"Amber Lynn. White trash stripper name, right? I met her when I was stationed in Alabama. Sweet southern girl but she kept my ass in check. Had this way of commanding me to do something while making it sound like my idea—some kind of southern Jedi mind trick. She had this hair, long blonde hair that went on for days. Totally cliché. She would sit on the edge of our bed naked, braiding it."

He hesitated, kind of coughed.

"She was pregnant when it all happened in Colorado. Not terribly far along. We didn't know what we were having. She knew in her bones it was a girl, though. She was so excited, glowing all over our crappy little house on base."

And that was all he said. We instantly dropped back into silence again. His rare verbal explosion disappeared into the air. Nothing but the snapping fire he lost himself into again. I wanted to ask what happened, but did it really matter *how* she died?

I could see her in my mind, this Amber Lynn. I envisioned her as stereotyped as she sounded. The long blonde hair cascading down her back, streaked with meticulous highlights to make her all the blonder. Tanning bed bronzed skin, feigning a sun- kissed summer. She would be thin and coyly sexual, allowing glimpses of her stomach to flirt between her shirt and the top of her pants. She would always be sufficiently made up, even for the grocery store, like a proper southern woman. Perpetually adorned with something shiny. I could almost hear a soft southern drawl slipping out from between full glossed lips.

Now the quiet felt awkward, painful, his wound left gaping between us with the imagination of her ghost trailing through my brain. I felt like I should reciprocate his disclosure; shift the subject from his dead to mine. I did not want to leave him exposed and alone between us, yet my mind no longer functioned conversationally. I could not access the past logically, I could not tell a narrative story. My past had been shattered and only existed in tortuous flashes among my memory. I could only dive headlong into a forgotten moment.

"I used to lie beside him, running my finger along this faint scar on his chest," I started. "It wasn't from anything exciting like getting knifed by a fleeing suspect. Just a minor training accident at the academy.

'I definitely tell people it was on the job,' he would always say. He said, 'You should have seen the size of this perp, I say.' We would just lay there laughing in our bed."

I lay there in that bed for a moment, feeling the sweet heat of his skin against my cheek, remembering how it felt to laugh. The way my shoulder would rock into his ribs as I giggled, the way my face stretched happily into a smile and I could feel my cheeks bunch up against my eyes. I wanted to bask in that perfect second just an instant longer before returning to the darkness with the fire moving between us.

Now that I had started, I couldn't stop myself. I didn't want to stop. I wanted to plummet recklessly into a million moments' stories and wallow in their echo. I wanted to conjure all the ghosts to come and hold me close against where we were, what we had done.

"Jordi," I almost choked on his name. I stopped for a moment and pressed my fist to my lips, willing away the menacing tears. "Jordi, my oldest, would walk beside Dante like an exquisite miniature. His broad shoulders and stocky strut scaled down and duplicated. Jordi took Dante's finger in his hand and they looked at each other grinning and swaggered on."

I smiled at the image of my perfect boys. My eyes dropped out of focus and let the picture swell over me. Again, for just a second.

"And Eli," I continued. I vomited up the past I had kept locked behind my teeth all these quiet months. "My sweet boy finally had some of me. Jordi looked just like daddy, but Eli had my eyes. My eyes looking back at me. He clung to me, always touching me for reassurance. He would run off and play then circle back to me, returning to base and pressing his forehead into my cheek before toddling off again."

I breathed out. I had said it. I had named them. I had acknowledged that dead and buried life for the first time in however many days, months, years. A part of me felt relieved, yet part of me opened up and bled again. I wanted to wrap myself up in their memories, but just the flash of them was already suffocating me.

He sat quietly in front of the flames with the sleeping baby folded in his lap. He had one hand on the child and the other holding up his chin. He stared vacantly into the flames, but I knew he had heard me. I knew he was filing away my words, analyzing them slowly. When I looked at the dozing bundle, I felt a flare of that betrayal, that outright anger at his decision. Yet even in my waning rage, I still wanted him. That familiar urge always rose from the ashes.

As the embers died and withered between us, twirling in our stillness, he gathered the infant in his arms and stood. I knew our routine; I knew it was time to find the softest patch of earth and try to steal sleep away from our nightmares.

We slept in the dirt with his body between us, just as I had done twice before. With another man. With other babies. He wrapped the child in his coat, placed his arm over the bundle, sword in hand. I eased tentatively beside them and lay rigidly against the ground. I knew I had to stay next to them; I knew that was our routine and it was expected, yet it had my body tensing and tightening.

As I lay there fighting the swell of maternal memories wafting from my very cells, the tiny hand found me. The sensation of the small touch caught my breath - I stopped breathing and could not move. My nerves stunned me. The child craved motherly flesh and the security it meant. I tried to pull away at first, tried to recoil into myself without being heard. Yet the child was relentless. He clung to my finger as he sucked his fist, and I wanted to die.

5

I awoke with the child's face nestled against my chest; his small skull fit perfectly under my chin and along my neck. I found my arm draped over him, cradling him into me. When my faculties sharpened and brought the world back into focus, I leapt away from the tiny snoozing body. He felt me startle away from the infant and lifted his head, saw me retreating sloppily as he kept his armed hand across the child.

The baby started to cry.

"Hey, hey," he spoke to me calmly, lifting a reassuring hand, as one would to a spooked horse.

I gathered all my limbs into my body and slammed my head against my knees, finding safety in the darkness. My heartbeat began to throb through my nerves and my ears again. If my eyes had been open, I was sure my vision would have been closing in on me. I knew the panic was painted all over me, evident in my flailing movements and frenzied breathing. I would have been embarrassed at my blatant display of emotional weakness if I had the capacity to give a single fuck. In this instant, it was a fight to cling to the island of sanity left in the sea of my mind.

"Breathe," he said coldly beside me.

I hadn't heard him move to me, but I could hear that he had collected the child and was rocking him, attempting to calm us both. The sound of his voice, his proximity to me subdued the outburst enough for me to start breathing again.

"I get it," he said. "Having Xavier is doing things to you, resurrecting too much of that life."

"Doing things to me?" I laughed. "You call this *things*. It's doing everything to me! I can't look at…I can't have him touch…I can't. I just can't."

He had no idea what it was doing to me. He could not see why I was so lost, why the existence of this child turned what was left of my world and my mind against me. He was incapable of seeing through my eyes. How could he when he had forbidden me from giving him any glimpse of myself since that first night? I was always alone right beside him.

"We are the lucky ones in this," he said softly. "You have to remember that. We can save him."

"Lucky ones? Are you fucking kidding me?"

"Yes. Lucky. We're still living, not like them."

"There's a difference between living and surviving."

The lucky ones. He was out of his fucking mind.

The lucky ones were decomposing happily beneath the ground upon which we marched.

The lucky ones never saw the end, never buried their loved ones.

The lucky ones did not survive.

He pulled the child in closer to him and leaned back on his heels. He waited for me to look up.

"Then why don't you do it then?" His tone sharpened.

"Do what?"

"End it. Kill yourself. We both know you want to. Why don't you get it over with and return to them?"

I hesitated, choked on the question. I had no idea what to say, though I had asked myself the same question every miserable day. I felt my face tighten and contort, fighting tears. I felt my heart sink deeper into my chest. He simply leaned his head to the side and waited for me to cough it up.

"I can't face them," I finally croaked. "I don't deserve them anymore."

"Why?"

"Because of what I am. Because of what I've done. They would not recognize me, and I wouldn't want them to see me."

"You're not like them. You're not one of those savages."

"Yes, I am." I paused. "And so are you. Somewhere in there. Unless you are the second son of God, we are all these savages. It's in all of us. It's just our nature."

"You can't think like that. And even if you're right, you don't have to give into that nature. None of us do. It's always been a choice, creature comforts or not. We choose."

"Then why are you the only one choosing to be human?"

"I'm not. You're choosing. He'll choose."

I put my head back down and just shook it against my knees. My words passed through him without impact. I could not sway his conviction, his purpose. And now he had this smaller piece of evidence to mold, to prove it wasn't just him. "Take him. I have to piss," he said.

I turned my head up at him, dumbfounded.

"Did you not just hear a fucking word I said? I fucking can't. It's too much."

He moved directly beside me, brought his face close to mine.

"Look at me," he said. "When you save a life, it is your responsibility. Whether you like it or not, we saved him. Both of us. We will take care of him. Both of us. Like I did once with you. I can't do it alone. You have to bury that shit and get past it because this, right here, is where we are."

I pursed my lips and stared forward. I could feel the tears burning my eyes. I felt like an angry teenager being scolded by her father, those same infuriating, frustrated tears and shaking hands. Me biting my lip just the same decades later. He had given me the only reminder that I couldn't dispute. He had saved me – I owed him my life.

I remembered thinking, is that a club? How cliché and caveman of it all. Then the impact split my sight. Pain poured over my skull as my vision sputtered and flickered. It hadn't been days since I packed the earth over the pieces of Dante's bloody body when I encountered them, the first I had faced alone.

I wanted to just let them have me, let it just be over. The weight of my abject apathy was like lead on my chest. Yet somewhere in me, a survival instinct persisted.

The three of them encircled me on the red dirt of the desert, panting rhythmically, one after the other. My head snapped between them, overwhelmed by the terrifying sound of their breathing. I could hear their tongues wriggling around at their teeth. I screamed wildly as I lunged at them with Dante's billy club, some failed intimidation technique. I could smell my own fear.

Then the club.
Then the darkness.
Between flashes of sight, I saw the dirt pluming around my face. In the blinks of the world, I felt blows raining down on me from every angle. My ribs, back,

shins, head, arms howled in the lightning storm of pain raging over my skin. I curled into the fetal position, closed my eyes, and pictured my boys on that last humane night, one man and two miniatures on a couch fighting over a huge bowl of popcorn.

Then it stopped. I heard the corpses pile up beside me. Then nothing. Silence. I cracked my eyelids and peered fearfully through my hands. Dead eyes and twisted limbs stared back at me. I lifted my head and faced the empty, glassy eyes. The three bodies were heaped together beside me, still leaking and settling. I tried to crawl to my knees, my nerves shrieked in objection. Every part of me cried out, but my body wilted in pain. He stood above me quietly, blade still drawn and dripping.

Without looking at him, I extended my arms. I tried not to look down as he gently placed the child in them. In the child's tiny body, I felt that he preferred me, the way infants gravitate towards females, that innate trust and plea for nurture. I could feel the nausea rolling up my body in waves. My arms begged to throw the baby away from me, to get that sickly comforting sensation of his small figure off my belly. I flirted with sanity as the surge of every tactile memory consumed me in one excruciating blur.

"Breathe. One…two…three… He'll come when he's ready," Goldilocks said, *patting the leg I could not feel. "All you have to do is breathe. Come on. Four…five…six…"*

I closed my eyes, and I breathed. In and out.

Concentrate on the breath. Release your thoughts. In and out.

One yoga mantra away from the brink. I breathed heavy and deliberate until my head stopped thumping and my heart stopped pounding. I had buried my three men. I could do this.

When I finally opened my eyes, the baby looked at me. His eyes stared distant and largely unfocused, like infant eyes, but I felt like he could see me. His pale skin had been unearthed when we cleaned him off the best we could. His sensitive skin remained red and wrinkled. He was waiting for his baby fat to flesh out his curled limbs and slender digits. The only blessing was that he looked nothing like my own babes.

He returned to us, though I knew he had been observing me first. I stood quickly and thrust the child back into his arms. He secured the baby in the carrier on his chest as we prepared to walk again.

The morning started in our normal silence. I found my comfortable place just behind and beside him. He held his sword firmly in one hand, yet the other rested on the back of the child. The babe was briefly awake, grunting and shifting helplessly in the carrier. I tried not to hear his sounds, tried not to think. The sun peered over the horizon, and I chose to focus on the colors bleeding up from the edge of the Earth. The sharp ball of light broke into the world, reaching bands of orange, pink, purple into the fading night. A few faint stars fought twinkling against the light until vanishing into the veil of day. The ground rose out of the darkness in the dim light, painted lavender and muted. Things could still be beautiful in this ugly world.

A forest sprouted up ahead of us, materializing first as a single tree then gaining numbers into the distance. It started at a point in the field then spread out over the horizon until all we could see were trees.

A forest was always a cumbersome and contradictory environment. The trees provided cover and camouflage yet opened up the opportunity for something else to hide from our view. Foliage concealed and trapped us simultaneously. It was an awkward mingling of comfort and fear, being at ease and on edge.

He breached the tree line first, steps ahead of me, still with one hand armed and one hand on the child.

I listened carefully for any sound—any rustling leaves, any cracking sticks—as open space disappeared behind us. The trees surrounded us and draped us in their shade. I monitored the minimal noise he made and continually compared it against the world, ensuring it was the only sound beside the light wind. Though we rarely had chatted on the road, we never spoke in a forest or an environment that neutralized the asset of far sight.

We were a few miles into the forest when I first saw it—a shape, a shadow flitting in the distance. Could be a trick of the mind, could be a figment of a nervous eye. I took a long, slow breath and kept my eyes locked to the left. I tightened my hand on my cutlass and tapped it quietly against my thigh.

Then I saw it pass between the trunks. A human head trailed by an arm before it slipped behind another tree.

"There's one of them up ahead. In the trees to the left," I said.

He stopped walking and looked to the left. We stood motionless and frozen until it showed itself again, just a glimpse, weaving closer now. He turned his head from side to side, surveying the area, assessing the situation.

"Good eye. Appears to be alone. Do you want to dispatch this one? My hands are a bit full now."

"They're always alone this far away from a city, it seems."

"Finally."

"Yeah, I don't miss the hordes. I'll get rid of it."

It had heard our low voices. It stopped moving for a moment, then I could hear it shuffling in our direction. *Yes, come find me. Make it easy.* They never ran, they always attacked. So much for a functioning fight-or-flight instinct. They always died.

I let the blade of my cutlass clang against the tree trunk beside me repeatedly. The child began to fuss behind me, where he was calmly watching, but I also heard the savage shift again. Closer. Then it leapt out from between the branches directly in front of me. It had been a man. Tattered remains of clothing clung to its waist, dirt and presumably blood smeared all over lean flesh. Its eyes were untamed and feral, and its mouth dangled wide among scraggly hair.

I stood and breathed calmly as it began to charge wildly at me. It let out a wheezing scream and held its arms wide, wrists slapping and scraping against the trees. I allowed it to lunge at me as I stepped to the side and let my cutlass slice through its arm. The limb fell dead among the foliage as it howled, recoiled, and came at me again.

It did not learn. I simply repeated my attack on the other side. As its clumsy body dove toward me, I darted from its path and brought my blade through its remaining arm. This time, it collapsed to the ground beside its two severed limbs, rolling around and looking desperately between the two lifeless hands, forearms, elbows.

I stepped over it and put my foot on its chest. The scars of fingernail marks raked down its face. How many people had it killed? Its eyes sunk in deeply, cheekbones jutting out, yet they bulged from deep in the sockets, always moving around in a frenzy. The lips hid beneath the plumes of beard; I could only see the yellow, plaque-ridden teeth. They snapped repeatedly as its black tongue wriggled behind them.

On its chest were the faded, flattened remnants of a tattoo. I thought I made out the sprawling wings of an eagle, but it was hard to see through the dirt.

Some deep and forgotten part of my mind wondered what it used to be when it was a man. I tried to picture it carefully and skillfully carving a Thanksgiving turkey at the head of a holiday spread— wife leaning in to assist as it separated the meat, candles lighting the smiling faces of children and grandparents. It would have worn a collared shirt and a hideous sweater vest. The sharp knife would have gleamed as it worked.

Yet all I saw was a gangly body lunge at Jordi. *Jordi cracked it hard in the jaw with a long stick, screaming "Get away from us! Get away from my family!" in his small voice. I felt a pang of pride in my panic. The creature howled violently as it retreated momentarily. Then it leaned in and snatched him up. I could hear my baby's screams as they were swallowed by the racing horde.*

Dante returned hours later, painted in blood, cradling the small, broken body wrapped in his shirt.

I closed my eyes against the welling memories and raised my cutlass high.

"Wait," he said from behind me. "Let me ask."

I sighed and rolled my eyes. "They don't speak."

He ignored my comment and stepped up beside me, bouncing softly to lull the babe. He asked what he always asked, knowing that even if they knew the answer, they would not or could not tell us. He crouched down to its face as it gnashed its flopping jaws and reeled around. He snatched the chin and held its face until it looked at him.

"What happened?" he asked calmly.

The creature only screamed in his face and dissolved into whimpers. It kicked its legs and rolled helplessly side to side. He reached down and seized the face again.

"What happened? Tell me what happened to the world."

Again, he was greeted with animalistic grunts. Its eyes were beginning to roll around inside its head. He sighed hard and stood up. I moved forward and plunged my blade into its face; it finally stopped writhing and moaning. He dropped his head down and let it rest against the infant's.

"What happened?" he said quietly into the soft hair. "When will we know what the fuck happened?"

"Does it matter?" I replied coldly, as I stepped on the head to pull my weapon free.

"Of course it matters. This was our world, their lives we lost. It matters what happened."

"But why? Zombies, plague, war. It happened, and it's over now. They are all dead just the same. It is all gone just the same. We are right here wandering around to nowhere just the same. Would you be comforted knowing?"

"Yes, I would."

"Wouldn't change a bit of circumstance."

"It would change me."

"How can you be this way? So unaffected. Still human in a world gone savage."

"It's human to ask why."

"As human as your extinct moral code."

"How do you do it?" he returned.

"Do what?"

"Just accept how things are, just abandon everything we were."

"You're the one who said we had no past, that it was all buried. You cling to these arbitrary rules from a civilization that is gone."

"That code is why I saved you." His words burned me.

"And maybe you shouldn't have. Would you have been better off if you had left me and were on your own all this time?"

We sat in silence so long that the conversation dissipated out of the present and started blowing into a memory as we stood over the lifeless savage at our feet.

"No," he finally said quietly, "I would not have been better off."

Then he slowly walked away.

6

Days passed awkwardly with the child. They no longer blurred together in a congruous string. Instead, they raked me over Time's coals, each second searing into my tender flesh before it finally rolled past. I lived straddling the infuriating present and the whirlwind of my past that it kept on beckoning.

For those clumsy days, I smoldered and festered at him. I turned my shoulder to him, avoided his eye. I refused to engage him; I only watched him fumble and flounder and learn childcare alone. He slipped the child into the carrier yet didn't notice the tiny leg hadn't made it out the appropriate hole until the babe screamed until he was red. He set the infant on his thigh for him to roll off into the dirt and dissolve into shrieks of panic. He fed the child, rocked him, tried to burp him—only for him to need a new diaper.

He did this to us – he could fucking figure it out.

Yet I found that half-hating him only made me want him more. What was wrong with my primal wiring?

My chest tightened when I looked at him, resentment coiling around my lungs. He had dragged me from death, resuscitated me, indoctrinated me for this. He told me then to bury my past to now beat me down with the reminders, with the one thing that had it all screaming through my brain. He convinced me to live just to get me fucking killed.

What the hell was he doing? What the fuck did he think he would find? In this pointless quest? In me? In this savage child?

The anger spread heat across my skin, tensed my muscles when I thought about it. The sensations pulsed over me in waves, animating all my nerves. Then I felt the flare, the carnal stirring in my core reaching out through my body. I felt my face flush and my nerves flutter.

Damn him.

"Why aren't there other children?" I asked. I had to break the silence; I had to distract my flesh.

"What?"

"Why is he the only child? Surely, these savages followed the prime biological directive. Surely, they fucked like animals. Why is he the only one we have ever seen?"

"I hadn't thought about that." He paused, shook his head. "I don't want to think about what happened to all their young."

He let the sound of our footsteps crunching over plants and twigs fill the space between us for a moment, then he spoke again.

"I remember the first time I saw a child in Iraq," he said. "I had been on base for weeks, seeing nothing but grunts. Then my unit finally rolled out of the wire, back into the fight. And there she was, a tiny alien sitting in the center of the road. She wouldn't move, no matter how we screamed at her and threatened her and pointed our guns at her. When we got out to physically move her, we discovered she was sitting right beside an IED. So we wouldn't run over it."

I didn't know what to say. I imagined that small girl in the middle of the desert road, dusty wind whipping her long black hair around full, dark eyes. I pictured her calmly not moving as soldiers with huge guns surrounded and shouted at her, holding to her purpose, saving their lives, risking her own for the invaders. The image, that idea shattered my reality for a second.

I was reeling, and he knew it. He stopped and looked back at me, tipped his sunglasses to read my face.

"Like I said, we're not all savages." Then he kept walking forward.

"You had to see more savagery in the Iraq war, though," I said.

"Of course I saw savagery. An entire country of savagery and desperation. If you push people far enough, they can lose all humanity."

"Then how is this a surprise to you? How can you think this could be any different?"

"Breaking point is a choice. Giving up is a choice. I met a man in Iraq, our 'terp."

"What's a 'terp?"

"Interpreter. He was an Iraqi, grew up surrounded by terrorists and murderers and savages. They found out he was working with us – it was a risk he chose to take. They slaughtered his entire family. In front of him. They burned his home, his life. They let him live just to suffer, knowing there was nothing he could really do to them. He could have gone mad. Maybe he should have. It would have been easiest. Yet there he was with us, making the choice to help us, because he believed things could be different. He believed his people could be more."

He stopped for a moment, his gaze growing long in front of him, falling into the memories.

"I used to ask him," he continued, "why he kept doing it, why he would pay such a price. He could have pursued revenge, he could have killed himself, he could have fled. He would say to me, 'I am not one of these animals. I know we are better than this.' I never really understood all he said at the time. But his words make more and more sense every day."

"What happened to him?"

"IED. He died in my arms waiting for the MEDEVAC."

And there was no response to that. A window had cracked open to his past, to his quest. He was fleshing out in front of my eyes. Was this my same stoic savior? Was this the man I had followed across all of these desolate lands? I never thought all of this lurked inside him. I could swim in his new depths.

The trees became thinner as we pressed on; sunlight broke in deeper and spread across us. Then the forest dissolved behind us, and we were back out in the open. It was comforting to see the circumference of our route, yet it was unnerving to be exposed again. There was no winning in this place.

The child broke our silence. It started as fussing, struggling against the carrier. Then he succumbed immediately, fully embracing the fit, throwing every ounce of his miniature strength into being heard. The piercing cry ruptured the sky, set my skin on fire. His little limbs flailed as his face scrunched down and turned red.

Then I saw it, down the hill and in the distance, a figure hobbling through the grass. Then another staggering behind it. And another hurrying to them.

"There, there," I whispered, gesturing down the hill. As I pointed, they turned to the sound of the baby shrieking. Another two emerged in the distance to join them. "Shit, it's almost a horde. Fuck, he's going to attract them all. Give him to me. Give him to me!"

I frantically stripped the small body from his chest and wrapped it tightly against me. He was already marching down the hill towards the group below, the baby carrier bobbing empty with his steps. He had his sword ready in one hand and the gun in the other.

I didn't bother to watch. I had seen him slaughter savages countless days in countless places. I looked down to soothe this damned infant who was steadily beckoning our demise. He was already calmer in my arms. He nuzzled against my chest, quivering his head and letting his open lips brush my skin. The little fucker was hungry.

With him cradled in one arm, I spun my pack around and dropped to my knees. I continued to scan around us and check his progress as I worked with my one free hand. I dumped some formula into the one bottle we had, splashed in water from my canteen, shook it quickly, and plugged the child. His whimpers instantly dissolved into ravenous suckling, and I felt that familiar victory in figuring out what the hell a child wanted.

I replaced my pack and looked up to see him striding back up the hill to us. Blood dripped from his sword, and his gun snuggled back in its holster. Behind him, a pile of pieces lay still and strewn over the ground.

"I think we can agree that it is your turn," he said as he wiped his blade in the grass.

I didn't reply. I merely allowed him to strap the baby carrier to my chest. I finally looked into his eyes – for the first time in days – when he nestled the child against me. I could feel the desperation in my own expression, the plea for him to not make me endure this. He met my eyes from behind his sunglasses and paused for a moment. He half-smiled in the necessity of it, brushed my cheek until he pushed my chin up, and then resumed leading us wherever the hell we were going.

I breathed in, breathed out, just focused on walking, and tried to ignore the tiny body moving against me, setting my nerves ablaze.

Too familiar. Too painful.

I dropped my arms away from the infant, almost held them back, arched my back as I walked. I looked up and tried to focus on the sky. The sun was retreating, shredding the blue sky, turning the trees and the grass red and purple. The wilderness was still beautiful. This was no bombed-out apocalypse. I remembered learning about the picturesque and the sublime in college literature. Not until moments like these did I truly understand how terrifying beauty could be.

Each step I took weakened my resolve; each step had my posture softening and my arms draping. The cells in my body were addicts, traitors to habits forged in two children. My shoulders needed to round protectively, my hand needed to huddle reassuringly. The memories in my flesh betrayed every attempt to fight the ones hammering in my scarred brain.

"He knows his momma," Dante said. "He'll always know his momma. Everything about you; your skin, your smell, the way you move, your voice is safe for him. He knows exactly the place to be. Used to be my place, little man, you better enjoy it." As Dante's words rocked around my skull, the child cooed and nuzzled his face into the skin of my chest. I only looked back up and let the hot tears carve canyons down the dirt on my face.

"Mom! Mom, look!" Jordi's small voice. "Look! I hold Eli. I hold the head. I good big brother." His smile practically cracked his cheeks open.

The memories were comforting knives in my heart. I wanted to close my eyes and lose myself in them, but I didn't think I could survive it. Every sound, every gesture, everything about that child sent ripples into waves out of my past crashing down on me.

The smell guided me back to the moment. I knew it well.

"Hand me one of those diapers," I said. "Only a few left. We need to raid again."

I crouched to the ground, and he stood over us, his calf against my back, weapon in hand.

I unwrapped the diaper to the both passive and potent stench of newborn shit. The loose, unnaturally colored pile smeared all over his tiny butt. I remembered tracking how many times my boys shit and peed, counting, evaluating color and volume, filing it in on the hospital-provided sheet.

I swabbed him with the backside of the diaper the best I could, wiping the castoff on my hands low on my pants. I cinched the tabs tight around his waist and replaced him on my chest. Before we started out again, I dug a small hole with our camp shovel and buried the diaper, just like I did with my own tampons and we did with our shit.

Must never leave a trail.

"How long do you think to the next town?" I asked.

"Can't be too far, probably camp tonight and find one sometime tomorrow."

"Then hope for the best."

"We can always improvise. People survived without disposables for thousands of years."

He started the fire then took the child from me as we ate from our prepper reserves. He looked at me differently with this baby between us. Perhaps he remembered the mother he fantasized his dead wife would be. Perhaps my past dripping all over me made me seem more whole, finally not vacant. Perhaps one tiny innocent made humanity seem possible again.

And I looked at him differently with the infant in his lap, cuddled up on his thigh as he ate above him. I tried not to look affectionately at the paternal shape of him. I tried to resist all the rosy images of Dante with our boys, the way fatherhood made me love him more, the way it added a whole other person to him. *Jordi stumbled on the hardwood floor, crashing to his little knees. His face contorted in soundless anguish—failure, pain, and fear twisted in muted tiny features. Dante took a couple jogging steps to his side and crouched down on the floor beside him. He pressed his large hand into the small back and leaned down to his son. I could not hear what he whispered to Jordi, but Jordi stopped, looked at him with wide and understanding eyes, wrapped his hand around Dante's finger, and stood to try to walk again.*

I fought the memories resurrected by looking at him and this child in the present, desperately trying to prevent the two from connecting, but my guts knew it was too late.

I wanted to believe it. Something withered deep within me wanted to think that this was okay, that this could work. I wanted to look upon the child and feel only the warm swell of mother in my chest. I wanted to fill that void in his life, be a little family, start over. That foolish part of me would get me killed; those dreams would only eat my soul.

That night, in the darkness, I heard the baby scoot softly across the dirt. I felt his tiny hand and cheek rooting out my flesh. As my nerves began to arch and writhe, I breathed deeply. I let the pain spread over and dissolve into me. Not Jordi, not Eli, I wrapped my arms around this child, gave him the only warmth, comfort, and protection I could offer. Alone in the dark, where no one could see. For my Jordi and my Eli, I did not shy away this time.

When dawn broke, the baby was still breathing sweetly into my chest. My shoulder and hip ached from remaining immobile on my side for so long, just as they always whined when I slept beside my boys for those precious hours strung together. The weight in the baby's breathing made it worth it, the way his toothless mouth hung open, top lip protruding forward.

He was almost smiling when he reached down and gathered the child. Without a word, he strapped the babe on, and we resumed formation.

7

The next town materialized nearly as he predicted as the midday sun beat down on us. This one was not as charming and seemingly preserved as the last. This one clearly bore the scars of demise. All of the outlying buildings had burned to the ground, and nothing but figments of foundations remained. Grass had started to reclaim the streets and lots, as if civilization had never beaten it back in the first place.

We walked in deeper cautiously. Every nerve, hair, and fiber of my being stood on edge. Instincts shrieked retreat and avoidance, but we could not risk neglecting some forgotten pocket of diapers or formula. Not now.

A rotting corpse dangled from a cross in front of what remained of the church, its arms spread in crucifixion homage to the plain, crossed white boards. Its bare skull hung to the side, the mouth agape in frozen horror. Flesh slumped and pulled toward the ground. All the blood drained and rotted long ago—if they didn't drink it. They had gotten to human sacrifice. Just when I thought there were no more horrors.

Forfeit just enough lives, and God will take it all back. Commit enough atrocities in His name, and He will just make it all stop. As if a deity would be so easily swayed from purpose and punishment.

"Jesus fucking Christ," I breathed. "When does it stop getting more horrible?"

He stopped and stood under the corpse, looking up at it and tilting his head as the child wiggled on him. At the bottom of the cross, below the decayed feet, something appeared scratched into the grain of the wood. The paint peeled back from the lines. I hesitantly stepped forward and reached toward it. Leaning back as far as I could, I let my fingertip trace the shape. It almost looked like a Z.

"Religious horrors are probably the oldest in the book," he replied. "Hell, they wrote the book."

"Is that supposed to make me feel better?"

"No. I'm only saying horrors are not new to whatever this is."

"Sounds like you're making my case for savagery not being new. Shouldn't God have taught them better?"

"We both know there is no God. We have to choose to be right on our own, save ourselves. God is not the reason. You shouldn't need a reason to be decent. Good doesn't count when you're only good for fear of punishment and damnation. Look how much they all mean it now. Those who are alive aren't even human anymore. Religion wasn't meant to answer the big question, it wasn't the opiate of the masses. Religion was invented to tame the savage. God is not a nosy deity, he was a prophet of behavior modification and manipulation; rewarded for good, punished for bad. Covers whichever incentive suits your personality type. Brilliant. Jesus wasn't the son of God – he was just the first mentalist."

"Hey, I thought you swapped your brain for a standard-issue cross tattoo and combat boots."

"That's what they thought. They do try to train it out of you, brainwash you depending on your MOS. But you can't put virile humans in survival situations and not expect them to thrive, adapt, evolve."

"Do you remember how they ran for the churches when it all started?"

"Yeah and I remember seeing a priest shooting at survivors in the street. Look how well it all worked out for them."

He gave the faux Jesus one more glance and sauntered away without looking back.

"I don't want to stay in this town," I said.

"I know. I feel it, too. One store and we're out."

"Is that like saying, 'I'll be right back' in a horror movie?"

"Let's fucking hope not. Horror movies? Really?"

"Yeah," I laughed. "My husband and I used to love the best of the worst. It was the only genre where something awful could still be awesome."

"I'll just have to take your word on that shit."

"Well what the fuck did you watch? No, wait, let me guess. Blockbuster action flicks. Oh, and historical fiction war movies."

"Of course. And the romantic comedies shoved down my poor throat every Friday night I was stateside."

"That's one way to make a man pray for deployment."

"You're telling me. But fuck, she was so cute. She would pop us popcorn, like on the stove and everything. And she would always cry at the end. You know, after they resolve the big miscommunication. I wanted to drink myself unconscious, but damn she was cute. Plus she always made it up to me."

Our voices bounced around between the remnants. This town was unnervingly quiet. We, for the first time, were not the silent element. Less safe in a more dangerous situation. What the fuck were we doing? The survivalist in me kept throwing up red flags, hazards, and warnings while my suicidal side just kept saying, *eh, whatever, come what may...*

We continued wandering through overgrown and dilapidated streets. The poor sacrifice in front of the church was not the only one. They had really tried. Crucified civilians plagued the city like 7-11s once did. They all rotted the same on the same perpendicular sticks. My heart sank into the cauldron of my miserable stomach each time.

I thought I saw another Z carved into a lonely wall, another formed from broken fence boards, another scratched onto the leathery skin of a hanging body. They seemed to be everywhere I looked, if I even remembered what letters and the alphabet looked like. The suggestion of cognitive humans was haunting, distressing.

"You think they're warnings rather than sacrifices?" I asked.

"Maybe, but I'm thinking sacrifices. It looks like this place was gone before the hordes started to migrate."

Good point. There were no bullet holes, no hatch marks in the walls that were still standing. Nature had a foothold far deeper than most of the other places we had seen. It was different, and different was always an extra layer of scary, something to peak the defenses all the higher.

"There are no fucking stores," I said. "I don't think there are any stores."

"No, let's bug the fuck out of here. Something is not right. We're not going to find shit here."

We were deep in what remained of the town, but we stopped dead in our tracks, turned left, and marched until the structures, half walls, and stones faded away behind us again. Every time I blinked, I still saw the crucified figures looming above me. Their twisted and elongated faces stared down at me. I felt the oppressive worry of my survivalist; I felt the heavy nagging stretch out uncomfortably into my limbs. The collapsed and burned-out buildings felt suffocating and menacing until they completely faded from my peripherals. My heart pounded savagely while I tried to pretend it wasn't behind us. It was under my skin, and I was not sure why.

As the natural world rose up around us and enveloped us in trees and grass, as the evidence of former civilization fell out of sight, my breathing slowed. My heartbeat calmed in my chest. I felt my arms lower back to my sides and my grip loosen on my cutlass. Blood was permitted to flow to my fingertips again. I looked to him and saw his shoulders return to their normal position. He slipped his gun back into its holster and released his clutch on the infant. We resumed default formation with only our minds remaining on edge.

"Why was that so creepy?" I said when the town miniaturized in our hindsight.

"Aside from the rotting human sacrifices?"

"Yes, aside from the obvious."

"I don't know. Something about how it seemed like it perished before everywhere else we've been."

"And that's a lot of places now."

"Yeah."

"Nothing like that."

"Yeah. The guts always know. Not the head, not the heart, the guts. Trust the guts."

"My guts say we're not far enough away yet."

"Concur," he said. The child whimpered and grunted into his chest. "Sorry, little man, we've got to get a little farther into the middle of nowhere."

The fields we began to traverse used to be farmlands. Fading crop lines barely remained between vegetation run wild. When we were far enough from the town that our hackles lay back down, we stopped on the rich soil, among the floppy leaves. I turned him around by the pack and gently slid my hands into the carrier to scoop out the small body. He didn't ask me to, didn't force the responsibility on me. He watched me for a moment as I wrapped the babe up in my arms and sat on the ground with him. Then he set to mix up the formula.

"I can't shake that town," I said. "I can always shake the town by the time it's out of sight." These used to be thoughts that were locked and restrained in my head.

"There's something different about this country, this direction. All of them have been horrible, equally horrible in different ways."

"Somehow, this one just feels different."

"Yeah. We're running out of options though. Can't go farther north than we've been, we wouldn't survive the winters nomadic like this. Going south wasn't worth trying, we couldn't push through that infestation to make it to Central or South America. Who knows what they are even like? East was stripped clean, the savages were just desperate. West is what we have. Maybe *different* will give us something."

I knew what he had in mind. He had never voiced it; he had never voiced much of anything before that tiny cry shook what remained of the world around us. I didn't see how we would find answers or proof or hope in a place that seemed even more bleak and lost than all the scorched places before it. To me, it felt like we were just descending deeper into hell, winding our way toward the end. I could look at the child without wanting to shear my skin and run away as screaming, bloody bones. I could look at him without a wild hate blooming in my stomach. Yet I still believed that this infant would get us killed, that we were just going to die off eventually just like all the others.

"Everything comes to an end. None of us can escape that. Sometimes you have to enjoy the ride to the bottom because that's all you have." Dante's voice quoted his father to me in what I once thought were my darkest hours.

I didn't give the child back either. I didn't rush for liberation. *Enjoy the ride to the bottom because that's all you have.* I attempted to slip on this mindset that never quite stuck in my previous life as I strapped on the baby carrier. The child burrowed into the flesh on my chest and was lulled instantly by the warmth. Once he was completely asleep, I let my lips graze the soft fuzz of his hair; I let my free hand press into his back. Shallow thoughts of my boys washed up around my ankles. How even in this filthy land, all new babies had that same smell. How all tiny wrinkled fingers looked grotesque and would be terrifying only if they were life-sized. How being preferred by a baby made me feel significant somehow.

I caught myself each time I felt personalization or affection flicker for the infant. My survivalist took diligent notes, but I attempted to breathe and just follow. Cautiously. I attempted to squeeze whatever fraction of non-misery I could before it ended up getting me killed.

As we lay down in our next camp, I pulled the baby in close to me. I didn't fight it, didn't make him wiggle laboriously across the dirt. The child's small body closer to me brought him closer to me as well. He still kept his armed hand across the child and the sword now rested on my leg, comforting and annoying at the same time. We slept entangled, the three of us, one mass of limbs and body heat. And the child slept soundly through the night.

When I awoke, he was still softly snoring beside us, his arm heavy over the baby and against my leg. However, the child was looking at me, *really* looking at me. He was changing daily, just as I remembered waking up to a new baby each morning with both of my boys. His eyes were beginning to track; he was starting to see more and more of this ugly world.

I looked back at him calmly. My heart pounded in my chest at the connection. My resolve wavered as emotions stirred and welled harder. *Breathe. Breathe.*

He reached up sloppily and bumped my nose with his tiny fist. I couldn't help but half-chuckle. The sound was foreign in my throat – I almost choked on it. The ridiculously mundane undermined the conflict swimming within me.

He stirred at the sound of my unpracticed laughter, stretching noisily then looking over at us.

"When I lost my babies, I wanted to die," I said abruptly. "I tried to lay there and slowly just waste away, wait for the next to come along and open me up. Dante dragged me along, managed to keep me fed and hidden. I couldn't look at him for weeks, he looked so like our babies. Then when I lost him, when he took that bullet for me, I couldn't do it. I couldn't kill myself and face them on the other side, couldn't forfeit the life he had died to give me. I waited, just waited for someone to do it for me, for it to just fucking end. But I found you instead. I got saved instead of slaughtered."

Then I stood and left them both lazing in the dirt as I wandered off to piss in a bush.

We were still meandering through farm country, though it hardly looked like farms and manicured crops anymore. The plants that grew unencumbered and naturally for however long now towered above us. Sunlight blinked between the stalks, the leaves brushed at our faces and rolled off against our shoulders and arms. It was not unlike the forest, yet this contracted environment felt comforting after that last town.

He had the child on his chest and moved to walk behind me to allow me to part our way through the plants. He shielded the babe, and I lifted my cutlass between leaves. As we pressed on, the crops began to thin. We could see the wide world around us again with only clumps of stalks randomly peppering the sprawling fields.

Without the pressuring leaves, he stepped around me, returned just in front of me and to the side.

"Switch?" he said.

I did not answer. I simply stopped walking and lowered my pack to the dirt. He turned to face me, reaching down into the carrier to extract the infant. His arms moved slowly along the sides, hands curling under the tiny body, making sure to collect the thin legs left dangling out. He was getting better at juggling the child, learning to anticipate the bobblehead and account for the inept little limbs.

He looked down when he interacted with the child, the only time he was not surveying and multitasking while he was awake. The baby stole instances of his sole attention. I would have thought such a feat was impossible. I didn't think anything could take him off mission.

Cradling the infant in his forearm, he looped the carrier over his head and handed it to me. I donned it quickly, tightening the straps and bringing the canvas closer to me. The child's eyes were open when he poured him into the pouch. He made actual eye contact with me for just a second, and I thought he might have smiled, but I knew newborns didn't genuinely smile.

Liberated from wearing the babe, he swung his sword through the air, loosened his arms. Then we set onward yet again. We moved into a large chunk of surviving stalks and plants, greenery coming in around us again.

The figure emerged from the shadows in broad daylight, just appeared from between the stalks without a rustle. My heart leapt into my chest as I lost my breath. One hand wrapped around the small body against me; the other raised the cutlass in front of us.

He was between the stranger and us in an instant, shoulders raised, gun pointed directly at him. The stranger simply looked past, large glassy eyes fixated on me. Then they drifted down and noticed the bundle cleaved to my body. His eyes grew wider still and flashed. His mouth fell open eagerly. He dropped his arms and leaned forward at us. Until the muzzle of the gun met his sweaty forehead.

"A baby," he rasped. He almost lunged, eyes agleam.

Words. He had said fucking words. We all stopped.

8

Our mouths both fell agape in the following silence. The stranger's eyes finally abandoned the child to fixate on the more pressing matters against his skull. And we froze there in the echo of speech for a long moment.

"What the fuck did you just say?" he finally said, gun unwavering.

"Ah yes," the stranger replied, raising his hands in official surrender. "They don't talk, do they? How long has it been since you talked to another person? Forgive me, my voice is a bit out of practice. Not all that safe to talk to oneself on the road. I'm sure you know."

His eyes slid to the side as he spoke, continually finding a home on the back of the child. For all his words, he could not keep his eyes off the babe, like a teenager confronted with an ample and exposed bosom.

It still seemed surreal to hear another voice. Our brains were fumbling around it.

"He fucking talks," I finally breathed.

"Yes, I talk," the stranger confirmed again, smirking. "I'm sorry. I'm sorry. The child there took me a bit off guard. I could see how my reaction was unnerving." He paused and waited for our reply, leaning his head forward and turning his ear toward us. "And you're not hearing a word I'm saying because I'm the only speaking person you've seen in who knows how long. You can see that I'm not one of them. Now do you mind with the gun there? My name is Uriah. My hands are empty. Let's just talk."

He slowly lowered the gun out of Uriah's face but kept a concentrated grip on it. He took a step back beside me, looking to me then the child before examining the stranger again.

"So talk," he said. "How are you the only one we have seen who can talk? Are there other survivors?"

"A couple," Uriah replied, standing more comfortably.

He shifted his weight from side to side. His eyes moved between the two of us yet always dropped, always lingered on the swaddled shape of the child. I felt my arms rise around tighter, holding the baby more protectively against my body. I wanted to turn my back to Uriah; I wanted to shield the infant from his very sight.

"We die off so quickly, as you know," he continued. The more he spoke, the more animated he became. "I started with a large group, running, scavenging. One by one, though. One of us got injured, cut real bad, infected. I left them a few days ago, continuing on to see if I could find something."

We no longer knew how to have conversations. We stood quietly in his fading words until Uriah began to fidget awkwardly.

He looked to me for some signal, but I had only doubt. I knew this was what he had been searching for; this is what he had dragged me over this forsaken land for—another survivor, one of "us." He kept his excitement carefully subdued. I could read it behind his eyes, but the rest was cold and unaffected. He wanted my consent for something, but I could only stare back at him as the wind licked my face and the child cooed at my skin.

"I haven't seen a child...since it happened," Uriah said.

"They died quickly," I said.

That shut him up. For a minute.

"Well, I don't really know where we go from here, my friends," he started again. "Haven't met any others."

"Let's make camp," he said, still looking at me, gauging my reaction, then turning to Uriah. "Camp with us tonight."

I tried to not let my face respond. Follow. Follow. Follow.

By the time we settled down for the night, the sun was setting and stealing the light away from us. He had led us, as he always did, to the perfect spot. I remained in my place as Uriah trailed me. I felt his presence scratching at my back. I couldn't round my shoulders around the child enough, couldn't grip my cutlass tight enough.

The small flames threw twisted shadows on our faces as we scraped soft food out of prepper cans. I felt Uriah's eyes on me as I took unenthused bites, as I put the dirty bottle near the fire to warm the formula mixed with the last of our water, as I held the child close as he ate. The audience made me uncomfortable. I would rather stand up and slit his throat than have him continue to stare at me, at the child.

Yet as my skin crawled under his gaze, I also studied Uriah out of the corner of my eye. He was long and lanky. His legs folded up beside him as he sat on a low rock, which somehow reminded me of a spider. His hair had clearly been growing unkempt for some time now. It dangled in brown strings from his scalp. He had been hacking back his beard though, leaving tufts of fluffy stubble across his face, aside from a bald spot of shiny flesh on his neck. I could tell he had been attractive in the last world. The symmetry in his features was still apparent from beneath the dirt. He had wide eyes and a straight nose with thin lips always moving beneath. His mouth unnerved me the most. Something about the way he smiled and talked out of the side of those thin lips.

His clothing was like all our clothing, just the tattered remnants. Stains blotted out any original color. Tearing and fraying betrayed any style. It was all just fabric, it was all just covering. He kept himself well covered though. Torn pants to his worn shoes, ratting cuffs to his dirty wrists. A few surviving buttons managed to hold his shirt together. Even through this threadbare mess, I could tell he had been very composed, very manicured once upon a time.

"What happened where you were?" Uriah asked as he ate our food.

He sat properly on the rock, ate as if he were at a table in a fine restaurant. Everything about his posture seemed purposeful. Nothing in his mannerisms was casual. He sat up straight, perched the can on his knees, and slowly spooned the food into his mouth. He even took the time to dab his chin with his shirtsleeve.

"Power outage for me," Uriah continued. "Lights, phones, water, everything went. People did okay the first month. Before they started changing. Before the nature came into it. Then it got ugly so quickly. It all just fell apart. And wherever I went, it had fallen apart there, too. What about you, my friend?"

This motherfucker never stopped talking. All those nights I wished for one other person with the gift of speech, and I wanted to cut out his fucking tongue and feed it to him.

"Illness swept the base," he said. He was suddenly quite chatty after months of silent steps and quiet days. "A lot of people died. Those who didn't were changed. It fell apart fast with so many available weapons and all their training."

"What about you?" Uriah looked to me. Yet again. "I never did catch your name."

"I haven't had a name for quite some time," I replied.

"Well she's the cryptic and dark one, isn't she?" Uriah said to him. "You guys must have really seen it out there."

"Blackout, too," I mumbled.

He looked over at me, knowing I was lying to Uriah. I remembered the first wave of transient savages breaking upon our town, the way people opened their doors to help them only to be ripped apart where they stood, the way they clawed at our walls and bashed at our windows.

"What did you do in the past life?" Uriah asked. I was not quite sure how he was managing to eat as he was constantly talking, constantly driving the conversation and questioning us.

"Army sergeant."

"Accountant." He looked at me again, counting another lie. He may not have known much about my past life or what I did, but he knew I was no accountant. I did not want to give this stranger one shred of truth.

"And you?" he asked Uriah.

"Television news anchor."

Uriah carefully set his empty can on the dirt beside him and stood. He looked down and took a breath then popped his head up, putting one hand on his stomach and extending the other welcomingly.

"Good morning, San Francisco," Uriah bellowed. "It's a beautiful day on the bay. Let's go first to Angela with your forecast."

"I lived a good life," Uriah blathered on. "Money, cars, women, minimal fame. As much fame as a news anchor has in the grocery store. Fuck, grocery stores. What I wouldn't give for one of those not rotted to shit. Just a nice deli sandwich. Thick cut meat, crusty bread, cheese, dripping with mustard."

They both leaned their heads to the side and let their mouths hang as their eyes stretched out into the idea. Even I could feel the rough texture of the bread grating along the roof of my mouth as I bit down and the contents of the sandwich slid around in my hands. My mouth watered, and my stomach protested the can of string beans.

"You know what I miss?" he said, joining Uriah's fantasy. "Beer."

"There is no need to miss beer, my friend. I happen to have some. I found it in the back office of an empty gas station, stuffed under a desk. Don't know why I didn't drink it then. Must have been saving it for now." Uriah beamed.

"How convenient," I mumbled. He shot me a look.

"Let me see," Uriah said as he rummaged through his sack. "Oh, I have four even. Do you want one?"

"Never was one for beer," I said. Yet another lie.

Uriah tossed him a beer. He plucked it from the air and sat musing at the can for a minute. His eyes wandered away as a smile played at his lips. More memories, more crumbs from that life.

The two men popped the cans and saluted each other before taking a long and clearly satisfying gulp. He closed his eyes, indulging whatever swelled up at the taste. I envied him that moment of escape. Uriah also threw his head back to fully embrace the beer. He eased up first, and his eyes fell on Uriah's neck as it undulated in swallows.

"What is that on your neck?" he asked Uriah, wiping his mouth.

"Ah, yes." Uriah reached up and touched the smooth, welted skin hiding under his long hair. "It is just a scar. Battle wound, you know."

"It looks kind of like a Z."

"Does it? I have never seen it for myself." He looked up as he fumbled at it with blunt fingertips. "I suppose it does feel that way."

"How does one get a Z-shaped war wound?"

"Well, clearly I was attacked by what used to be Zorro. Some habits never die!"

He slashed a Z into the air with a nearby stick. They both laughed, and I rolled my eyes.

"I have my own war wounds," he said as his laughter died out. "Not from this war though."

"Afghanistan?" Uriah asked.

"Nah, Iraq." He lifted his right pant leg to reveal the marbled, welted flesh spotted with tufts of leg hair that I had seen and silently questioned since the first time I saw him bathe. "IED," he said curtly.

Then they were quiet, momentarily sullen. Why was he telling him this? He had never told me this in all our days and survivals. I had seen the scars, and he had told me nothing. Yet here he was confessing his entire buried life to this stranger. Was he going to tell him all about his dead wife, the one tidbit I had extracted in all our wanderings?

"Family?" he asked Uriah, smiling again and looking down at the can in his hands.

Now he was asking for stories of the last world, actually digging up the pasts he insisted on entombing. I felt my chest tighten. I could feel my irritation tingling in my hands. He never cared what I had lost.

"No, no. I was a bachelor," Uriah said. "A single career man. You?"

"No. Too many deployments, you know." Now was his turn to lie.

"Just an ex-husband," I said shortly.

"Ah, maybe it is the single who survive these days. Quite the reversal. Hard to tell with most of the others, you know. They are no conversationalists. But then who is this baby?" I hated how he looked at the child, the way his eyes seemed to lick his lips. "Yours?"

"Yes," I answered by reaction.

"Ah, love on the road," he laughed. "So humanity marches on. He could be the beginning of the repopulation," he said, lifting his beer.

I heard the two empty cans hit the flame as they tossed their empties, then they cracked the second round. My very blood begged for just a taste of the numbness I remembered, especially with the twisting pressure blooming in my chest the longer they talked. I could not get comfortable. I could not settle into my skin around him; I could not smile. My eyes lingered on the ground as he shared all I had always wanted to know with this outsider.

"You remember how it was before it happened?" he said. His tongue wagged loosely in his head now. "Everything was about the goddamned apocalypse. Every movie was about zombies –there were reality shows about doomsday preppers. It's like we knew."

Drunken philosopher. My road prophet. The longer they talked, the more I felt like I was with two strangers.

"I don't think the fixation was all about the apocalypse, though," I finally chimed in. I could not let them wander away completely without me. "I think it always was more an examination of what happens to people when society breaks down, without civilization, what we become in those more natural circumstances. I guess no one figured we'd go this far, though."

My words broke upon him, but he did not move or react. As always. Then he shook his head for a moment, seemed to find himself again. He didn't acknowledge what I said, didn't grant me conversation. He just continued on with Uriah as if I was not there at all.

"So you've been coming from the west?" he asked.

"Yeah, I started in the west, obviously," Uriah replied. "West is cannibal country, though. You been through Vegas yet? Nothing but a crater. People scurrying around it naked, like ants. Terrifying bug-eyed, gangly creatures. Long ago, back when there were others who spoke, I heard they bury their kills in a mass grave in the center of the crater, where The Strip used to be. Guess you can't be surprised that a place like that went to hell. But I've been all over in these years, running, migrating, searching. They don't speak anywhere anymore. In the south, they just grunt. Like animals. Crawling around on all fours. The zombies."

He smiled at Uriah's manners and his willingness to blather on about the different subtypes of savages, but something in Uriah's every word made me bristle. Something in the way he smiled at me out of the corner of his eye made my very guts flinch.

"North," Uriah said. "I'm heading north. Maybe where Canada used to be."

"You've got a long road ahead of you that way," he said solemnly.

We both fell silent for a moment. I knew he saw my bloody beaten body, heard me begging him to just let me die when he dragged me back to where I started. There were only graves behind us to the north.

"Have you ever heard what happened?" He finally asked it, what he always wanted to know.

"There were many theories at first. You know, before they all died. Everyone had a story from where they were. I heard some sort of degeneration of the brain is causing us to devolve. Virus or biological warfare. Zombies, of course. Then nothing at all, that this was us all along." He looked at me when he said this. "I've found no answers. If anyone knew, they are long dead."

He hungrily drank down the information, parched from his isolation with me. Being around someone who cared, who knew anything, animated him. I watched myself being replaced with each word, watched him seduced by the possibility of camaraderie. I shifted awkwardly and out of place, shuffling with the child against me.

"What do you think happened?" he asked Uriah.

"Me? My personal opinion? At first, I thought it had to be some disease. There was just no way people were like this, that this was us. But the longer I looked at them, the longer I ran from them. I don't know. Maybe this is just what we are." And he looked into my eyes again.

My spine tried to leap out of my back at that look in his eye. I felt a wave of nausea tease at my throat. The child could feel the change in me; he could read my discomfort and started to fuss. He didn't feel safe against my tensed muscles and cringing skin. I stood and held him against me, turning and walking away from the fire. I held his tiny body up near my face and hushed him. Suddenly, he felt like my only kindred spirit in this empty night.

I could still hear them talking.

"You don't like that theory?" I heard Uriah ask.

I knew he hated that theory, rejected it to his very core.

"There was always savagery." Uriah continued yammering. "People shooting up elementary schools, people scamming others out of every cent to have more money than they could ever spend. Hell, I made my living selling and sensationalizing it on the news. One that really haunted me was a mother who burned her children alive. Locked them up in their house and just set it on fire. Then she played it off as just an accidental house fire, just a tragedy. She was collecting money from all these charities; the community was rallying around and helping her. Until the investigation concluded. She pled insanity of course. They always did."

"One of the worst I remember was when on my second tour in Iraq. We busted this terrorist cell in Baghdad. There was a woman involved, not in charge obviously, but still running things. She was having men in the group rape the women so she could then shame them into blowing themselves up as suicide bombers. She told them it was their only chance to regain any honor."

Uriah fell silent for the briefest of moments. I could feel the quiet of the night for an instant. My own uterus cringed as I felt that same crushing sensation in my chest that weighed on me every time I heard just one more awful thing.

"That is a particularly upsetting one," Uriah said, sipping at his beer again. "But with all this, what you have to ask yourself, my friend, is were we ever really civilized? Could we call any of that civilized? Or was it something we just told ourselves and pretended at? Sure, we were smart enough to think so, but were we ever truly more than animals underneath it all?"

"No, I don't believe it. We're not them."

"We are what we are when no one is looking, and we have always been murderers, thieves, rapists, and animals. It's not that we became something else; we simply devolved into what we have always been. Civilization was just a flickering illusion. Turn out the lights long enough and you see what we really are."

"Not all of us. You can't generalize and say all of us. Even if we are born animals like you say, everything else is a choice. We choose to be good."

"Which makes being good all the more extraordinary. We just never saw it with all our lighted, dancing distractions. Those who were good are dead, my friend. Survival doesn't favor the civilized, clearly. It's too bad the good people didn't survive. You couldn't survive this and be a good person. One had to be sacrificed. Tell me, if something threatened those two, would you not turn savage, too?"

"That's different. Defense is not savagery."

"Semantics, my friend."

If he said *my friend* one more time, I was going to drop the child, sprint over, and tear his head from his scrawny neck. Then how savage would I be to him? Would he execute me for slaughtering his new comrade?

I knew I wasn't good; I was already dead; I had died twice in Chicago and once more somewhere in the desert. There was no goodness left in me when I watched the life fade from a baby's eyes that looked just like mine. I wouldn't have wanted to see what this world would have made my boys. I didn't know why he insisted I was like him; he always thought I was something more than what I was. Maybe that's why he kept me alive and kept me close all this time. Some imagined glimmer of hope. There were only so many times I could tell him what I was. He saw what he wanted.

He clung to his humanity, clung to me as evidence of it. I was a walking, breathing reminder that he could still be selfless, that he could still care. That obligation held me close to him in a cold, sterile binding. What he felt, I could never really tell. It didn't matter. Survivors only felt guilt, fear, and regret anymore. Anything else was a memory in those buried pasts. I wasn't me to him; I was what he needed me to be to remember himself. I let him sacrifice the truth of me a little—tax on the debt I owed him.

"But you can't dispute the elegance in the nature of it," Uriah said, his irritating voice snatching me back from my thoughts. "The sheer fucking brilliance of Mother Nature. The only thing that could finally start to kill us off was us. The evolutionary poetry of it."

Their words had emotions smashing around inside me, colliding with my cells. I rocked away from their babbling until the light from the fire began to fail and the edge of shadows curled around my boots. I looked down at the baby's face I could not see in the dark and let my finger trace his cheek. If it got dark enough, if I closed my eyes tight enough, maybe he could be Jordi or Eli just for a second. Maybe I could be the mother that did not fail them just for a breath. His crying subsided as I looked up into a sky full of stars that I never saw through city lights.

The crunching of footsteps brought me back. I recognized his shape against the small flames behind him. I could make out Uriah still seated on the same rock. I bounced the child out of habit until he reached me. He stood so close to me, wavering, that I had to look up at him. His features were a mystery in the dark.

"What's with you tonight?" he asked.

"Nothing. Just calming him."

"Why did you lie to him?"

"I don't know. Something about him."

"He's the first we've met. You're just on edge."

"Maybe. It's strange, being around another. Just doesn't feel right."

"He's proof that it's not just us. We can't walk away from that."

"What are we going to do? Adopt him, too?"

"We're just talking now. But we might want to go with him, find those others."

"There's just something not right about him. Something about the way he looks…" I stopped myself.

He took another step forward. The alcohol changed him: he lingered. His chest bumped into my shoulder as he swayed in his own boots.

"You know I won't let anything happen to you," he said softly, down into my neck. I felt his hand rise up along my back but then heard it fall back alongside his body.

I looked up into the black of his face, arms still wrapped around the child.

"He needs to sleep," I said. "I think you need to sleep, too."

"Okay, Amber," he slurred.

I tried to not let his wife's name cut me in half. I tried to just breathe past it until it fell out of the moment. I had to take care of him and the child. I knew somewhere deep in my guts that I had to keep them close to me tonight.

"Uriah!" I called, not looking away from his rocking form. "We'll see you in the morning."

"All right," he hollered from the fire. "Good night!"

Good night. Such foreign and forgotten pleasantries.

He walked sideways when I slid my arm under his and guided him. His body weight swayed against me as I tried to balance him and the child. I led us until I felt safe, far enough away. When I stopped, he wobbled to his knees. I slid the coat from his shoulders and wrapped the baby up and placed him gently on the ground.

As I set the child on the dirt, I felt his hand at my hip. He guided me to my knees beside him. In the dimmest light, I could make out a lazy smile across his lips. His fingers stumbled along my cheek, and his exhales plumed alcohol against my face. I held my breath, waited. Then his body lurched to the side. I clutched his arm and leaned back to counter his fall. Struggling and shaking, I eased him to the ground beside the child.

"Thank you," he kind of laughed.

I heard him turn to his side. His weapon scraped the dirt as he drug it up and around the baby, draping his arm over the sleeping body.

I collapsed with a sigh onto my back beside them. I could hear them both breathing in the dark next to me. I listened to make sure I heard nothing else before my mind slipped off the edge of consciousness.

9

I woke up to screaming, baby screaming. For the briefest of moments, my half-sleeping brain held me in bed with Dante snoring beside me as cries echoed down the hall from the nursery. Then I felt the dirt under my cheek and remembered where I was.

I instinctively reached for the bundle. It was nothing but a crumpled coat. His arm was still over it as he snored passed out—a heavy, lazy, drug-induced breathing.

By the breaking dawn, I could see Uriah struggling, shushing and trying to wrangle the irate infant. I could make out the wild look in his eyes and the desperation on his face. *Must make it quiet.*

He tried to wrap his arms around the child, yet the babe fought with every fiber of its little being. He squirmed and screamed and bucked. Uriah's inexperienced hands fumbled and failed to get a grip on the tiny body enough to flee with him.

I could read the panic in his face; then, in an instant, it changed. He snarled, and aggression extended out through his movements. He lowered the babe to the ground, practically dropped him to the dirt, then began clawing at the ground around him for something. I was already sprinting. Before I even saw him grasp the rock, I was on top of him. I dove at him and turned my face to avoid colliding with his. I let my chest deliver the brunt of the impact into his shoulder and send him flying back away from the baby.

The child continued to squall beside us as I tackled Uriah. Our bodies flopped onto the dirt, and I heard the breath rush out of his body as my weight slammed against him. Dust flew up around us in a cloud. He reacted like an overturned turtle, arms and legs shooting out sloppily. I kept my body rigid, concentrated on keeping him incapacitated, on punishing him. He pushed and kicked until he writhed out from under me and forced himself upright.

He came at me in a flurry of limbs and snorts, untrained and unfocused. He grunted and threw a blur of careless punches. I could have rolled my eyes at his incompetent attempt. I breathed calmly and dodged the impacts, turned his momentum against him. My fury brought me clarity, unleashed my training. He lunged in desperately to grab me. His eyes were wide and wild, his fingers pathetically anxious. I took hold of his arm and contorted it until it folded against him, wrestling him down to the ground. I kept thinking, *he's one of them.*

He continued his inept fight, bucking and snarling. I moved on top of him and crawled up his body until I could firmly press my shin into his throat. I deprived him of the air required for his wasted exertion. I knelt and pushed until his fingers clawed at and dug into my thigh, trying to lift me. Then I reached to the ground beside us and took his rock high in my hand.

"No," he said from behind me.

I whirled around, still pressing my weight into Uriah's neck until I could hear him choke. He squinted and staggered as if hungover and shuffled to scoop up the shrieking baby, sword dangling amongst his fingers.

"He was going to kill Xavier," I said heatedly. It was the first time I had said the child's name. "He's one of them."

I saw lucidity flash in his eyes. His posture straightened as he calmly rose up in himself.

"Take him," he said.

I let the rock roll from my fingertips and dug my leg into Uriah's neck again as I stood, wrapping the baby close in my arms. He was wailing, still panicked, thrashing his tiny body and groping at me with inarticulate hands. I curled my body around him and attempted to envelope him back into some illusion of safety. He pressed his hot cheek firmly against my chest as he sucked at his thumb so hard I could hear it.

When I looked up, he was standing over Uriah. He dragged him up from his back and to his knees.

"You're just like them," he snarled. "You're one of *them.*"

"We're all them, my friend."

Uriah coughed and rubbed at his throat. His demeanor had changed. Everything I saw in his eyes lay out wide in the open, poured out over for him to finally see. Uriah abandoned his prim composure, and his body regressed to a more primal stance—shoulders rising and rounding, head sinking. He knelt there, before the sword, calm and snickering. He mocked him with his eyes now.

"She knows." Uriah nodded at me, stared directly into my eyes, then turned back up to him.

"Why?" he asked Uriah.

Let the interrogation begin.

He kept his sword up and at the ready as he paced around Uriah. Uriah remained on his knees before him as he took long steps and kept his head down, Uriah always in his sights.

"Why what?" Uriah asked.

"Why did you approach us? Why did you take the kid?"

"Why not?" he laughed. "What possible reason would there be to just watch you and your little whore march on past with that little morsel?"

He tensed twice as Uriah spoke. Subtly, but I saw his hackles rise. His rhythmic pace hesitated. He breathed out as he forced his shoulders back down and resumed his steady circling.

"How many of you are there?"

"Me? Just the one."

"No. The savages."

"*Savages*. Such a stupid word for it. Haven't you noticed? This whole country is what you call 'savages'. You think you're so much better than me, so much more evolved." His tone turned from mocking to bitter. "Holding onto a world that's dead and gone. I'm a *survivor*, my friend."

Not for long, my friend. I was ready for him to die. I knew his patience wore thinner each time Uriah spoke, but I also knew he would milk Uriah until he was dry of any viable information. Anything to know. Anything to help us survive.

"I really did come from San Francisco," Uriah continued. "After it all went to shit, I did drift and scavenge and scrape. I was barely surviving when I found them. When they found me. A horde of them here in the middle, picking off the wanderers. They didn't speak, but they saw what I was, knew I was one of them. Then living became much easier."

Maybe he was telling us this because he knew he was going to die. Maybe he was telling us because we were the only other ones with language. Maybe he just liked to hear himself talk.

"What did you give me?" He ignored the answers, filed them away in his mind, and pressed on questioning Uriah.

"Little of this, little of that. Not everything from the old world is completely lost."

"Have you seen any others like us? Killed any others like us?"

"Of course. Been killing them since it all fell. Just waited for stupid survivors to come through. They were always looking for the answer, always wanting a friend."

"How recently? Where?"

Uriah fell momentarily silent with a smug smirk painted across his weathered face. He stepped forward and snatched Uriah by the neck, pressing hard until I could hear Uriah's breathing struggle.

"Tell me!" he yelled as his composure wavered.

"It's been years, my friend." Uriah laughed. "You are all dead."

Uriah looked sideways up at him, twisting his neck in the grip until he could look into his eyes. He tossed Uriah back and stepped away.

"Do others talk?" he continued.

"Wouldn't you want to know? But you're like me, aren't you, sweetheart?"

He looked past him, focused on me again. He leaned to the side, arching over on his knees to burrow his eyes into me another time. He tried to rape me with his eye contact, tried to pry into me, that sideways smile still painted hauntingly on his lips.

"Saw right through me all along," Uriah said. "We always know our own. Deep down, at your core, you know what you are, what we *all* are. We could make tons of delicious little babies together." He licked his lips disturbingly.

He stepped in front of Uriah and blocked his view of us until Uriah looked back up at him.

"They eat their own young," I breathed, clutching Xavier closer.

"Why would you eat your own children?" he asked Uriah, disgust betraying him and creeping out into his tone. "You're just going to die out."

"Just like you. Just like everyone else. You ever think this whole mess is just Mother Nature finally saying *enough* to her viral infection of humanity? Open your eyes. She should have made God wear a rubber."

What the fuck was he saying? With his mask ripped aside, savage insanity poured through his practiced charm. His true nature exposed.

"And now you think I sound crazy," he laughed, "which you'll turn into another justification for executing me." Laughter swelled up in him until he doubled over in chuckles.

We both stopped and just watched him cackling to himself. When his snickers finally faded, he straightened up again and brushed the tears from his dirty cheeks.

"Will you be any less savage after you do this?" Uriah said to him, giving him that slicing look he had been reserving for me. "The only difference is what you tell yourself. The only difference has always been what we tell ourselves."

He just kept talking. And talking. He never stopped *talking*, and I was tired of listening. I bounced anxiously, waiting for him to just fucking do it already.

"Whether you plunge that blade through my heart to eat me or to righteously defend your family, you still plunge that blade through my heart," Uriah continued. "My blood wets the ground just the same. I die just the same. And as I'm rotting, none of your reasons will matter; none of them will change that you killed me."

He stopped, paused for an instant for emphasis. He looked at me out of the side of his eye to spill that crooked smile in my direction, and then he shot his eyes back up to him. He slowed and dropped his voice.

"Like a savage."

The next sound was his head hitting the dirt. It made a heavy and satisfying thud. As his skull rolled across the ground, the sideways grin remained plastered across his lips and his greasy hair spun out around it before settling to the soil. His inanimate body followed separately, toppling forward from the knees. His arms dragged lifelessly behind and splayed out over the earth. I felt satisfaction at his severed head falling, at his quiet body collapsing. I felt reprieve when it was finally silent again. The mother tigress flared in me.

He stood unmoving over the body for a long time. His sword hung in one hand as he lowered his head to his chest. I watched his shoulders rise and fall with heavy breath, but otherwise, he was frozen. Xavier nestled hard under my chin, the fatigue of his fight winning over him.

I waited, savoring the resolve, appreciating the win. The truth was revealed, the threat was neutralized. I felt relief, but I knew he did not share that sentiment. I knew something much more significant had been ripped from him. Uriah had amputated the hope from the back of his mind. I wanted to place my hand on his shoulder to comfort him, yet at the same time, I felt slightly justified in his regret. He had discarded me and trusted this stranger so easily; he had ignored every instinct I had. His decisions had led us here.

"You thought I was one of them," I finally said softly. "You thought I was going to kill the one other person left like you."

"He had me fooled," he replied simply.

"He told you what you wanted to believe."

"Yes."

"What was he? He wasn't like the rest."

"An evolved savage."

"Like us."

"No. He used his intelligence to enable the savage. We use it to avoid it. You are the only one left like me."

"None of us are like you anymore. I was going to kill him, bash his skull in with that rock."

"I did kill him. Killing is not what makes us savage."

"Isn't it? Isn't justification our only difference? Like he said."

"You loved Xavier today. You weren't going to eat a human child. Nothing is more human than motherhood."

"Nothing is more savage and base than motherhood."

"It's dawn. Let's get the fuck out of here. Leave this fucker to rot."

Those were the last words we said. The crumpled body and head faded with each step into another traumatic memory, his great hope spun away in the wind. He didn't speak for hours. There were only the sounds of our footsteps and the child's cooing. I kept Xavier; I didn't even ask. My hand still pressed into his tiny back, my shoulders still rounded him into my body. We just followed him silently. I wanted to console him, tell him it would be all right, but I didn't think it would be.

He had deflated in front of me. His shoulders slumped as his arms just dangled from his body. His head bobbed side to side as it fell forward and hung to the mercy of his steps. I recognized what defeated looked like, what betrayed looked like, what regret looked like. I knew the horrible gnawing sensation that was pressing on his chest. I knew the weight that was now packed into his legs and how heavy his head had suddenly become. I knew how embarrassing it was to endanger your family.

This was the wrong time to think about wanting to press my skin into his, but as always, I thought it just the same.

We put miles between us and Uriah's remains. No matter how far we made it, it was still painted all over us in his blood splattered on our clothes, in our slouched forms. He took us at an accelerated pace. I felt him trying to outrun the mistake, trying to forget the freshly cemented memory. We didn't stop to eat, didn't stop to rest. I mixed formula and swigged off the water as we moved. I knew this is what he needed, so I powered through as my exhausted muscles threw out pain flares.

It wasn't even dark when they attacked us.

The sun had just begun to flirt with the horizon when they materialized from the distant trees. There were so many of them, more than my brain could initially assess. Their dark shapes poured out from between the narrow trunks. They didn't stagger, crawl, or sprint; they marched to us smoothly and with purpose.

They *thought*.

As my heart pounded and the adrenaline surged through my veins, I saw him snap back into himself. Combat training at its best. His head lost its weight and settled back into its correct placement. His shoulders rolled up and back. His arms stirred and began speaking with his weapons. He sidelined his failure, separated from it, and simply went to work.

There were too many for him to handle alone. I could not spectate as I had been able to since that fateful day we found Xavier. I would have to fight— with a baby strapped to my chest. I would have to defend myself and kill with an infant vulnerable over my heart. I felt a wave of something familiar rage up over me; it pounded in my eyes. I hadn't felt genuine, body-shaking fear since my last boy had died.

"You can't think," he had said to me in the desert. *"You can't think about what you're going to do, if you're going to die, that they might injure you. You can't think about the families they used to have. You can't think about the people they used to be. You can't think about what your family would think of you. You cannot think. The training is in your bones, in your muscle memory. That is your sanity. Don't think – just do."*

I took the risk of closing my eyes and breathed in deeply. Then I lifted my cutlass and my gun and chased after him.

10

I closed my eyes again and listened to the sound of my own panting. My heartbeat thumped in my skull, almost causing my teeth to bump against each other. The only other sound was that of cooling combat, rasping death moans, dripping blood. I dropped my head back and looked at the sky first. Twilight painted the clouds as light started to wane. Another long breath before I pulled my head up and turned my eyes to him.

The swarm littered the ground in pieces and bloody fragments. He studied one severed head. He crouched down and leaned closer, eyes squinted and head cocked to the side. Then he popped up horrified and hurried to the next closest corpse. Then again and again. Confused, I stepped forward to the first head. Something on the neck caught my eye. I moved in and squinted to see a familiar welted and shiny scar that looked just like a Z.

He finally stopped and stood among the mangled corpses, weapon still raised in his hand, and closed his eyes.

"They have the same scar. They have the same fucking scar," he said. "He was one of them. He was their fucking scout. How could I not see it?"

As the adrenaline faded from my head, I felt my own body again. Something warm and wet was on my stomach. I looked down into the carrier. Xavier lay still against me, eyes closed as if he were sleeping. Blood poured down my pants. My body only said, *not mine*.

I released my weapon from my fingertips, but I did not even hear it drop to the dirt. I reached up with a quivering, vacant hand and gently touched his face. Nothing. He did not move. I could already feel him growing colder.

"He's not moving. Xavier's not moving." I cried.

A familiar panic flared over me. It radiated through my limbs. I suddenly felt trapped, suffocated with this tiny corpse strapped to me. Eli's empty eyes just like mine staring up at me.

"Dante, he's dead. Dante, our baby's dead. Eli! Eli!"

I dissolved into a blur of flailing and shrieks. My mind seized with memory. *His tiny face was green. I didn't know how a child of his color could be green. I had never seen such a horrifying shade of green. He wrestled with his discomfort, whimpering and groping for me. Even though I had him cuddled tightly to my chest, he did not feel me. He searched desperately for me, crying for the comfort I was supposed to be able to give him. His tiny limbs trembled, and his body shone with a thin veil of sweat. He started to shake harder. Another seizure was coming. The tears were already in my eyes. My arms ached in helplessness, cried in paralysis. I sobbed as I clutched him to me. I wiped the foam slipping from his petite mouth. Then he stopped. But he did not move again. He went limp in my arms, and his little mouth hung open.*

At some point, he pushed through and managed to strip Xavier from my chest. He cradled the small body when I resurfaced sobbing in the dirt. He just looked at me. His face held no expression, hidden behind those goddamn sunglasses. He was a statue watching me flounder on the bottom.

I couldn't force my body to stand. I was only aware of the vacancy on my chest, of the pool of blood soaking the front of my clothes, of my paralyzing failure. I rolled to my back in the dirt, rolling on top of my pack, and allowed myself to weep. The sobs crushed my eyelids down and blotted out the clear sky above me. I had no words to say, nothing I could do. The only answer was to fall apart among the severed pieces of the savages that put us here.

At some point, his footsteps begin to move away. The retreating sound brought me back to the dirt. He didn't speak when he turned and began to walk. He didn't even look back – he knew I would follow, scraping and sobbing behind him. I dragged myself painfully to my feet and trudged.

He carried the body as we walked, keeping all the limbs tucked tightly against him. I knew he was looking for the perfect spot. In a field, he found a large, lonely tree. Wavering grass stretched out on all sides as the tree towered above and looked down on it. It was a landmark. It was special. We moved into the shade of the twisting branches as he surveyed the ground below.

He placed Xavier gently on the grass, very slowly lowering him and ensuring his little arms and legs were properly folded against his body. Then he turned and started digging with the camping shovel we used to bury his diapers. With a tiny mound of soil beside him, he took the swaddling coat and meticulously lined the grave with it. Then he gently placed Xavier in on the coat and wrapped him as he did when he slept between us.

He knelt there for a long moment, hands in the dirt on either side of the hole. Through my own tears, I thought I saw a tear or two trace his cheek. He leaned down and put his lips to the dead infant's forehead.

"I'm sorry, Xavier. This was my fault, my blindness. Sleep well, little man."

Then the shovel scraped, the dirt fell, and my sobs grew. I no longer cared for his composure or his moral code. I no longer cared what I owed him. I howled wildly and threw myself at the small pile of earth. I dropped to my knees beside the tiny hole, digging my hands deep into the dirt, raking my nails until I felt the grains press into my nail bed. It couldn't hurt enough. I watered his bones with my tears, tears for other small corpses long rotting.

Jordi ripped apart by savages as he tried to protect us, buried in a baseball field of what was once a school. Eli wasted away by a disease I could have never imagined, burned for our safety while I couldn't watch, and then scattered into the nearest open field. Dante shot in front of me, stealing my death and giving me this life I didn't deserve, hastily covered with loose desert sand because I didn't have the strength to give him a proper burial before dark closed in. And now this tiny square under this isolated tree, burying my last attempt at humanity.

The pain aching in my mind was excruciating. The shredding sensation ripping down my center was too much for me to endure. He had done this to me. He had brought us here. I just needed it to stop. I lashed at him, throwing a fury of wayward blows.

"Why? Why would you make me bury another child? Why would you make me love and feel all this again? Why do you keep me alive for all this suffering?"

He raised his arms to protect his face but allowed me to slam my arms and fists into him. Finally, he caught me by the wrists, whirled me around and restrained me with my arms, wrapping me in a straitjacket of my own body. He did not hold me tightly, he loosely gripped me until the fight dropped out of me.

"He was *ours*. His is our loss," he said into my hair.

He released me, and I simply let myself tumble back to the ground. He stumbled away from the small grave, turned away from my crumpled, sobbing body. Again, through my tears, I saw him stagger, the liquid bending the light and distending the world. He placed his hand firmly on the trunk of the tree and cast his eyes up as the branches swayed in the gentle breeze. The sun had abandoned us, and only its fading aftermath illuminated this horrendous scene.

When his back was to me, I slowly reached into my pocket. I took out four green Army figures. They had been with me every day since Jordi's broken body; they had pressed into my thigh when I lay broken on the sand of the desert. *"This one here, with binoculars, that one is Daddy. He's always looking around. And this one here with the big gun, that's me. I protect us. This one on his belly is Eli because he doesn't walk. And this one, Momma, this one holding his gun up, that can be you."* I clenched the tiny men in my hand as Jordi's voice echoed in the wind. Then one by one, I pressed them into the dirt above Xavier with my fingertip.

He stood frozen for a long time, like a memorial statue, until my neck strained from craning up to watch him. Then his elbow betrayed him. He jerked. I heard myself gasp quietly. He didn't even attempt to catch himself. He just allowed his limbs to fold and collapse until he stuttered against the bark and slid rigidly to the ground.

He flopped down on his back in the sound of tumbling gear. His arms and legs toppled beside him until he was as flat as a corpse. I had never seen him lay down except to sleep. He rarely sat, his arms were always engaged, hands always to purpose. Yet there he was, lifeless and breathing.

I knew what was happening to him; I knew what he was doing. A part of him nestled deep against his heart was falling away to crawl into the soil with Xavier—that part of him that loved the child too much to leave him alone in the ground. That piece was dying, committing suicide. It would leave a gaping wound that I had thrice in my own soul. I knew the darkness that was welling up in his chest. I mopped the tears from my cheeks and went to lay down in it beside him.

He did not look at me as I shifted to parallel him – I knew that he could not. Aside from the pull of the pain across my puffed, welted, and wet face, he was tumbling deep from behind those eyes. I eased down with him, flat on my back, and watched the leaves move as my eyes lost focus and tears continued to burn tracks down my cheeks. I strove hard to think of nothing at all.

"You were right," he finally said. Darkness consumed the sky above us. His voice tangled in his throat.

"No," I said without moving. "I wasn't."

I heard him shift as he finally heaved his head up from the dirt, breath whisking out from between his dry lips. He rolled onto his side, turned toward me. I felt his fingers press into my chin as he gently guided my face from the sky.

His sunglasses were off. I did not often see his eyes. I looked into them even less. Something about that connection was intimidating. They were blue, dark around the pupil and pale at the edges. They were swimming in unconsummated tears as he just stared into me for a moment. I could feel those eyes in the pit of my stomach, pressing against my very core.

"I'm sorry," he said.

I couldn't say anything.

His eyes wavered. He looked at my mouth. I thought I saw his teeth tug barely at his bottom lip. The sunlight had completely diffused out of the sky as it pressed down upon us.

"We stay with him tonight," I said, looking down and stumbling on my words.

I dragged myself to my feet and reached down to collect him up. His hand found mine and held it as we moved. We lay on either side of the little grave. He draped his sword over me now as his other hand kept mine and we tried to sleep with him between us one last time.

11

Again, I cried for days as we walked. Just as I had three times before and every day spent grieving them.

Again, he led, and I followed.

He silently offered me more of his canteen to replenish dehydrating tears. We didn't speak. He walked, and I wept. We had lost together. Not as Dante and I had lost together but as close as I could get with dead sons. It was not like killing together, it was not survival. It was crawling down into the same hole to wrap up in the same pain. I realized it wasn't the fight that bonded soldiers – it was the fallen.

The cutlass dangled heavy in my hand. I let it slip in my fingertips until he heard it bouncing on the dirt. He stopped and turned to me, lifting the blade and carefully resting it against my shoulder. He let a calloused finger graze the tears from my cheek. Then we walked on.

"North?" I asked.

"We've been north. Plus, we wouldn't make it far before winter hit. We continue west."

"We can't go west. You heard him."

"We have to go west. It's all that's left."

There was nothing west. I knew it. There was nothing anywhere. I didn't know I could lose any more, yet somehow I was still granted the horrific privilege. New horrors every day.

I kept seeing Uriah's face and that twisted smile. My skin continued to crawl at the thought of it. I tried to focus on how satisfying it was to watch that stupid head fall off his body, neck planted in the dirt.

"Z? For what? Fucking zombies?" I knew we were both thinking it.

"No. Anything with a pulse that wants to eat other humans is nothing but a cannibal."

"You think they were like him? Evolved savages, like you called it?"

"No. Not one of them said a word. None of them were smart enough to win."

"Neither was he."

"You saw through him. These were not the savages we've seen, but they were not him, either."

"A whole fucking spectrum now. Lucky us."

I couldn't do it. I couldn't just have a conversation. I couldn't just keep marching on. I could feel my face writhing as another wave of pain crawled up my body. As the tears began to burst out of my eyes, I turned and just stormed away, walked fast and hard without looking up, without any direction. I found a tree and pressed my forehead into it until I felt the bark threaten to pierce my skin.

I hadn't heard him follow me. He stopped. I heard him breathe out slowly, heavily. I felt his hand lightly touch my shoulder, and he turned me to him.

He had never touched me. He had restrained me in role-play as he trained me to fight in the desert, he had snatched my hand or arm to drag me as we ran, and he had fumbled at me before collapsing after Uriah's beers;

he had never touched me for sake of physical contact or comfort. With his hand still on my shoulder, he looked at me. He had never actually looked at me before, never maintained eye contact long enough to connect with me. Even at Xavier's grave when the pain blinded us. He had never really seen me.

I stood frozen, confused, staring back at him. What was that foreign look? Was it good-bye? Was this my mercy killing at last? Could his buried savage look at me so sweetly?

He wrapped his arms around me, brought me close to him. I closed my eyes and collapsed into him, yielded myself, surrendered. I pictured them, my three boys, happy and alive, and waiting for me. I smiled and knew he wouldn't let it hurt that much to get me to the other side.

Yet he just held me. I felt his hand smooth down my hair and his mouth against my scalp. I felt the tension in his muscles as he truly clutched me to him.

"Not that easy, Parker."

My name.

I hadn't heard my name in another's voice in an eternity. The sound of it sent memory charges blasting in my head, stirred an old version of me. I felt myself sobbing against him as darkness fell around us.

12

I woke up flat on my back on the ground as the sun started to pierce the sky. His arm rested across my hips, sword clutched in his hand. He was on his side, still dozing. His bottom lip dangled, and I could hear his breath playing through his teeth. I felt the weight of his arm on my body and thought of Xavier between us. I looked at the vacant scrap of ground and felt my heart contract. I closed my eyes and tried to remember how to forget a child.

The faded farmlands had disappeared behind us. That lonely tree and tiny grave only haunted our memories. Another fallen, another left behind.

My heart wanted to think about Xavier, Dante, Eli, Jordi. My soul wanted to sink out of my body and into the ground with them. There were too many ghosts, we were outnumbered. The feeling of his arm against me, the sound of his breathing pooling in the dirt beside me was all that kept me grounded in the flesh.

I wished I could have rolled over and pressed my face into the warmth of his neck.

"The mountains are coming," he mumbled.

I rolled my head to look at him. He had not moved. His eyes still closed, and his hand still draped over my body.

"Yeah?"

"Yeah. No way around them to get west. Then to the desert again."

"The desert where we started?"

"No, not exactly. But close. I'm not sure we would have made it had we not stumbled on those prepper rations."

We both fell silent for a moment, trying to forget what else we had found there. I felt the heat of tears filling my eyes.

"Only problem is the pass," he said as he finally stirred and sat up.

"How's that?"

What was this conversation shit? What was this discussing the plan? My voice barely knew how to communicate this much anymore, but I finally didn't feel so claustrophobic trapped alone in myself. There was no space between us anymore, no silence. There was no point with what we had lost together.

"Smartest course would be to take a road," he said.

We hadn't set boots on a road or a street outside of a city since he found me. The point was to avoid any vestiges of civilization unless stocking up on supplies. Stay away, stay hidden. Avoid the savages.

Maybe there wouldn't be savages scouring a remote mountain pass. It would be less likely than an abandoned four-lane interstate. But I understood the risk: exposed in the open, walking down the skeleton of the societal empire.

"So we risk it," I said.

What did we really have to lose anymore?

He rolled up onto his feet and stood beside me. I looked up and found his hand waiting for me. It confused me for a moment, those dirty, outstretched fingers wavering in the air beside my face. My own hand remembered the protocol. I let my fingers slide along his calluses as he gripped and pulled me up beside him.

His fingers lingered around mine, as they did when we slept beside Xavier's grave. He loitered just inside my space, as he did the night Uriah drugged him. Time hesitated in our suspended animation, as it did every time he was near me now. Then he released my fingers, and we just started walking on, as we always did.

Each step brought us higher, inching up in altitude, ramping up in incline. A seemingly endless sea of waving prairie grass began to climb in the distance, aspiring into foothills.

"They aren't Colorado Rockies, but they are still damn beautiful," he said as the horizon began ascending in the distance.

Beautiful was a strange and foreign word. For all the sublime images I glimpsed in the wreckage of our wanderings—stepping onto a silent carpet of wildflowers so vibrant I had to squint, heat lightning snaking up into thunderheads over the desert after I buried Dante, a million stars stretched by my tears consuming the sky in the absence of light, the sunlight being split into sharp rays by the remaining shards of once mighty buildings—the sound of that word remained almost mocking of the fallen out world through which we trudged. Yet in these steps along the culmination of continental collision, it did feel appropriate. The Earth rose up high above us, reminding us how insignificant we were, how easily we could be lost and forgotten as these rocks remained unchanged and unaffected. They had witnessed species rise and fall long before our pathetic demise.

"So how do we find this road through the mountain pass?" I asked.

"Ever since Manifest Destiny, there has always been a way west. All the way to the coast. We'll just have to chase a little civilization, trace the highways out of the next town at a distance until we have to use them to cross. It's going to get cold. Even though it's not winter. The altitude."

"Like hypothermia cold?"

"Unlikely. More just uncomfortable nights."

I couldn't remember the last time I had a comfortable night.

I felt that altitude gaining on us the farther we moved. Each step had my perpetually fatigued muscles working harder to march me up the increasing slope. Long, stale grass and lonely yucca plants bowed to exposed rock and trees. Walking became climbing. For all my following and slaughtering, I did not have mountain lungs. My body insisted I note its many tiny objections.

My chest still felt vacant without him snuggled there. My body had not adjusted to his sudden absence. It had been so hungry to replace the stimulation of motherhood, it was reluctant to release the brief figment I had only just embraced. I felt a hole on and inside my chest. My shoulders felt light without the carrier weighing them. I caught my hand wandering up to rest on his back that was no longer there.

We snaked around trees, weaving our way upwards. The sky peeked down at us from between piney branches, sun winking among the shadows. Then the trees broke. The ground leveled to birth a clearing, small and isolated.

"Is that a lake?" I said.

"Yeah. A little one."

"I need a bath." I tried not to conjure up visions of a warm, frothy bubble bath with candles, wine after the boys had been fighting me the entire day, and Dante downstairs wrestling them into exhaustion. I just wanted to be clean, to wash the film from my skin.

"Gonna be cold." He almost laughed at me.

"Do you remember the last time I had a bath?"

"Uh, the last time we saw a river. Weeks before that town. River wasn't that clean, either."

"Exactly. This even looks clean. I think I'll brave the cold."

The world smelled clean up here where the air was thin, where the wall of pine trees enveloped us. I could see in his demeanor that he was home, the way his body language spoke to the environment, the composition of the Earth around him, in a familiar tongue. I could see wanting this mountain to be my home, right beside this lake, where we could pretend the world below us did not exist.

I slowly stripped off all my layers—dirt, dried blood, regret—and left them piled at my feet. I felt the air embrace every part of me, and for the briefest of moments, I felt free, reborn. The tempered liberation of being naked.

My body was not what it was in my other life. What had once been rounded hips and a gentle belly had disintegrated into leaned and stretched flesh. My bones jutted out from the pale and dirty skin; my muscles strung tightly between knobby joints. Emaciated was a word that played in my mind as I let my eyes actually wander the foreign landscape of my own form for the first time since I had a mirror in my safe little home.

I had always hated my body. Since adolescence, I stood before my reflection, wrinkling my nose as I took handfuls of skin wherever I could. My stomach was too soft; my legs were too short; my hair was too wavy; my face was not symmetrical enough. Now I longed for the stubby legs I remembered, for the healthy belly I despised, for the hydrated skin at which I relentlessly picked. I never appreciated the beauty Dante saw in me, and now it was as dead as he was. I was the walking corpse of that woman.

I fully envisioned my old body, my true skin one last time. I permitted myself to remember the way Dante would smile and wet his lips when I came out of the shower all nude and dripping.

I took tentative, naked steps across the ground until I felt the damp shore beneath the soles of my feet, followed by the bite of the crisp water. The cold was abrupt, abrasive yet somehow welcome. The longer I wriggled my toes against the cool temptation of paralysis, the more my skin relaxed into the sensation, embraced the temperature. As the water pooled around my ankles and I felt the clean chill climb my legs, I looked back at him. *Just join me. Just touch me.* He looked down and purposefully trudged off to accomplish something. I let sliding steps on the slippery lake bottom guide me to the deep. Then I let the water consume me. I felt revitalized as the shock of the cold resonated through my entire skeleton.

As I floated aimlessly, breasts and knees teasing the surface, I did not think – I did not *remember*. I only mused at stray clouds meandering across the forgotten sky. The water started to feel comforting, and the air tickled my wet, exposed flesh into chills.

Couldn't I drown right here? Couldn't it end just this easily? Peaceful for once.

When my skin started to sag waterlogged from my bones, I dragged myself back to the parched shore. He had returned and continued to busy himself. I stood at the water's edge. And waited. Water snaked down my bare flesh as the wind licked me into goose bumps. And I waited. I felt my skin tighten and contract. I heard the water splatter from the unkempt ends of my hair. I felt droplets chasing the curve of my hips.

I waited until he looked at me, then I just stared at him. *React. See me.*

My catatonia made him uncomfortable. He dropped my gaze and tried to fumble back to whatever fake task only to find my naked stare still lingering. I began to air dry. For once, he didn't want to face me. For once, he didn't want to confront me. For once, I intimidated him. Yet I could not keep retreating. I could not keep wrestling my hungry flesh. This time, I waited.

Finally, he stood, eyes to the ground. He reached down and flipped one of the meager blankets I had clawed out of Xavier's swaddling closet. He stepped slowly until he was square in front of me and, without looking up, wrapped me in the blanket. Slowly, meticulously, he draped the fabric over my shoulders and pulled it around me.

My eyes burned into his face, but he refused to meet them. He hesitated there before me, with his fingers still tangled in the edges of the cloth. His chin twitched up then recoiled. Then he did look at me. One long, heavy look as he leaned into me.

I felt his breath on my face as my eyes fluttered shut. Then he was gone. I heard his steps crunching away as I held the blanket naked, wet, and alone.

Rejection was a punch in the chest. I felt all the air leave my body as I was left gasping for it. Stunned, I kept my eyes closed for a long time so I did not have to see his back as he walked away from me. I don't know what I expected in all those times I fantasized about consummating my desire, yet this reaction left me hollow and aching.

I pulled the blanket tighter around myself, felt the dirty fabric destroying my momentarily clean skin. I surrendered and shrank down to the ground.

I dressed and already had a small fire burning not far from the water when he wandered back out of the trees. I coiled tightly around myself, hugging my knees into my chest, resting my chin on them. I did not look at him when he approached. I felt the anger stretched thinly over my face, I felt the rejection burrowing into my chest.

All of the waiting for him to wrap me up and walk away from me. He did not want me. I was not good enough, even when there was no one else.

"Let's have it," he said, sitting beside me and staring down.

"What?" It was difficult to unclench my teeth and force the word out.

"I know you're pissed."

"Do you? Why am I pissed?"

"Come on."

"No. I've just been rejected by the last man on earth. Why would I be pissed?"

He breathed out slow and long. I still didn't look at him. I remained wrapped around myself, trying not to let the pain show, trying not to care. I felt that same dead weight of rejection as I'd had against a junior high locker as my first real crush walked away.

"You know," he finally said, taking his time and speaking slowly. "You have to know. I would not save you, not from them, not from becoming them, not from yourself, if I didn't love you."

My mind abjectly refused to interpret his words. They filtered into my brain then faded back out. I only heard that he didn't want me. I only heard that he had left me standing there so vulnerable.

"You think I'll become one of them?" I asked. Maybe he didn't want the savage in me.

"You think we are all them already."

"You love me, but you don't *want* me?" I had no reason to be coy anymore. I let the thoughts fall out of my mouth unfiltered.

He laughed. "Yeah, that's not it."

Laugh? How could he fucking laugh at this?

"What? Sex is savage, too?" I snapped.

From the corner of my eye, I saw the stiff smile fall off his face. His features slacked, and he stared forward silently. He breathed deeply for a long moment.

"I still see her face," he finally said quietly.

Now, I could say nothing. I choked on my rage. My contempt broke for a moment, and I looked over at his now stoic form. Every cell in my body knew what he meant. Dante haunted my every step.

"When I look at you now," he said, "I see him. Him sleeping on your chest, him in that hole."

Again, he spoke words that resonated in my own soul, echoes of my own torments. *Dante nuzzled up against me by dying firelight. He wrapped his arms tight around me, put his chin into the curve of my neck, kissed my skin. I could only lay there and stare into the embers, haunted by Jordi's broken body and Eli's green face.*

It was the last time I could have made love to Dante.

He shifted on his seat and turned to face me. He looked at me, and I looked down as he started to speak again.

"My wife never saw me pull the trigger until a target stopped moving. She never forgave me for slaughtering half of a village to come home to her. She never knew this part of me, this *savage* as you call it. I used to worry in the desert. I used to sit in that horrible fucking green light inside an MRAP and worry about what she would think of me if she saw me, if she *knew*. That thought almost got me killed more than once. I don't think she could have loved me through this."

"You'd be surprised. I loved Dante every bloody second until he died. Except when he retrieved Jordi and burned Eli. Then I hated him for giving them to me at all."

"This. This is easier. This is training. Light the fire, kill the food, kill the threats, walk. How do you go home after war? How do you step back into a place where it seems like none of it ever happened?"

My anger had dissipated. I couldn't think about sexual denial or his rebuff with talk of our dead still burning my lips. It was trivial again, it didn't matter again. It had always been foolish.

There was nothing else to say, no words to fill the now awkward silence.

As the sun abandoned the sky, all the warmth in the air contracted into the tiny flames. I felt the thin bite of the night air against my face as chill nibbled through my clothes. My skin quivered first before the tremble migrated into my muscles. I clutched myself tighter as I heard the shiver in my own breath.

"I told you it was going to get cold up here," he said. "Come here."

I looked over at him out of the corner of my eye. He lifted his arm to encourage me over. My flesh wanted to leap into him, but my wounds restrained me. The many times I had wanted to dive into him, and now I hesitated. I huddled against myself and turned back to the fire.

"Stop being such a girl and get over here. It's all about the body heat. You can go back to being pissed in the morning."

It was damn cold. I looked over at him again. He opened his coat, and I couldn't resist. He welcomed me in, spreading the blanket over us and wrapping himself around me. I pressed my nose into the fabric of his shirt, felt his warmth on the texture of the fibers. His scent wafted over me, the smell of the dirt we trudged through, the sweat long dried on his flesh.

"My wife used to have this three day thing," he said into my hair. "If I pissed her off, which was often enough with how stubborn we both were, she made me suffer for three days. Three days of cold shoulders and snippy comments, maybe even the couch. Then it was over. On to the next."

How could we ever really live a new life if all we saw were flashbacks of the ones we lost? How could I be anything more to him with the ghostly memories of his dead wife always pluming around me?

13

The road felt strange beneath the soles of my boots. Unnatural. We had not traced it out of some mountain town like he had planned. Rather, we had just stumbled upon a forest service road. The trees halted, and our footsteps crunched on gravel. The sound was unnerving, almost deafening on the silent mountainside. He led us along it, chasing through the vegetation and pinecones along its winding trail, until it spilled us onto asphalt.

The lonely veil of civilization felt intrusive upon our wilderness. I found my body recoiling. I didn't want to walk on it; I didn't want to be anywhere near it. The survivalist in me kept reminding me of the hazard, of the exposure. Even if it was colder and more remote up here, they could still be teeming. I didn't like it, didn't trust it, but I followed him. Just over this pass. Then we could slip back off the grid again.

We didn't speak of the previous night. We didn't speak much at all. He was on alert as we stepped into risk; I was trapped somewhere between what we had lost and what he had denied me.

When I tried to lose myself in the present, I found myself thinking how much I wished I had seen these mountains in my past life. I could imagine driving our white crossover SUV through the winding curves, silhouettes of the trees echoing off the windshield, snow teasing in the air. Jordi and Eli in the backseat in ski hats, sharing a tablet between them, watching some cartoon. Dante swirling his finger around a map on his smart phone.

I apparently could not live in the present.

He strode just ahead of me, locked at attention. He had his shoulders rolled back and down, drawing his head up straight at the summit of his spine. One arm engaged his sword, keeping it tensed and ready. The other teased at the butt of his gun, flirted with it, reminded it they would play again at any moment. He looked the most in his skin in moments like this. The fight was his element. Threats gave him something to understand and to deal with. I only complicated his simple survival.

"Are you still mad?" he finally asked as we crested the pass.

The world opened up and sprawled out below us. The view was breathtaking; I could see the mountain range lazing out to our sides in random peaks. The mountain sprawled down from our feet and splashed out into the distance, rippling in foothills. Miles unfolded exposed and naked before us, unable to hide or conceal from our vantage point. I allowed myself to come to a complete stop for just a breath and truly see it, feeling superior for the briefest of instances. Our boots turned downward and marched into the horizon falling off in the distance. We could abandon the treacherous road now and descend in cover.

The miniaturized terrain shifted and changed in colors and textures, like brushstrokes on a painting. I felt like I could reach out and run my fingertips along the transitions as I always had the childish desire to do in an art gallery. I could see towns glinting in the landscape below. I could even see the desert menacing the edge of the mountain terrain, peeking out in the hazy distance, crouching and stalking us.

Straight ahead and far away, I could make out the forgotten silhouette of a city. At the sight of lines so branded and ingrained in my memories, my heart seized. I had always preferred the urban lifestyle, felt at home in the concrete jungle. I wanted to take the L to a Cubbies game. I wanted to find pizza after last call. I wanted to be bumped by strangers hurrying down the street. I could barely make out the shape of skyscrapers glinting in the sun, yet my mind summoned the comforting sight of the Chicago skyline reflecting off the water. The structures beckoned me on an instinctual level, somehow suggesting they could be safe and familiar once more.

"No," I said as we weaved between trees again. And I even believed I wasn't. "It was a stupid moment."

He stopped walking and turned back to face me. "Not stupid," he said.

I didn't want to look at him. I didn't want to connect with him over unsuccessfully throwing myself at him. He pushed his sunglasses onto his forehead.

"Look at me," he said. I reluctantly turned my eyes up to meet his blues. "You and me. Stay with me. Nothing changes. West."

"Westward, ho."

He smiled, slid his sunglasses back down, and led us on.

We were walking away from the city, yet it still grew as we moved farther down out of the mountains. I caught my eyes wandering in their direction every couple of steps. I kept correcting my boots to follow him, to stay on course just a few feet behind and to the side. I felt the sun on my face and heard the soft splashing of the fountain in Grant Park. I heard the footsteps of a jogger falling beside me, the rumble of a bike tire on the asphalt. I heard Jordi, *"Look at the flowers, Mommy."*

I bid farewell to the trees and the grass and the plant life as the dirt and sand gradually overwhelmed the ground below us.

I could feel that distant city on the side of my mind as we walked, pressing against my focus, whispering to my resolve. I thought of St. Patrick's Day in downtown with the river dyed green, Dante and I in a proper pub cloaked in dark wood. The sounds of people—real, living, breathing, civilized people—echoed in my mind, chanting out an Irish drinking song. A wave of isolation swelled in me so far out in the wilderness, so alone with only him beside me. My chest throbbed to climb back into that city memory and tuck it in around me.

Back in the desert. How long had it been since he had found me in the desert? Dante and I had just wandered, ran, fled in any direction. Anywhere away from our dead babies, from where we died as parents. Farm bled into prairie bled into mountains bled into desert. The dry dirt crunched under my feet, and I remembered it felt appropriate to be somewhere so barren. As dead as I felt.

"We need water if we're going to get across this desert, babe," Dante said as I trudged behind him.

"Where are we going?"

"South, I think. Maybe it's different in Mexico. Maybe there's something."

The desert was too familiar. Like a crying infant in my arms, it plunged me headlong into a history of demons. The present was burning at the edges, going dark as the past lit up before my eyes.

"Is the desert doing it?" his voice broke into my fog. "Bringing it back?"

I didn't want to think about what he would remember from the desert. He would see me waiting for three savages to slaughter me. He would see me completely broken, in a lumpy puddle on the sand. He would hear me sniveling uncontrollably for days, sloppy and drunk with grief. He would hear my raving, calling him a cunt, begging him for death. He would remember me at my lowest and most desperate.

His hand found my shoulder. He turned me to him.

"Don't fight it," he said calmly. "Just let it come and let it pass. Talk to me. Tell me."

I breathed ragged and desperately as he eased me down beside him, brimming flashbacks continuing to menace me.

"They weren't savages," I started. "Not like these now, at least. They approached us in the desert. Spoke to us. Like Uriah. Talked about what happened where they were, how they thought it was some disease related to the government. Conspiracy theory shit. They lulled us into complacency. It wasn't hard. We had just buried our sons and neither of us was very sharp. I was the fucking walking dead, only stumbling on for Dante. I couldn't take his whole family from him."

I stopped. My tongue shriveled and glued to the roof of my mouth. I choked on the memory as it began to swell high over me.

"They turned on you," he said for me, throwing me an anchor to the moment, to him.

"Yes," I sputtered. I never thought I would be telling this story. "Just before night fell, in the twilight, while we tried to scrape together food. They had their guns on me, knowing Dante would do whatever they wanted. They took everything. Our little food and water, our bags, weapons. All I had was the club in my hand and the Army figures in my pocket. As they were turning to leave us to starve or get maimed by the next horde, one of them turned back."

I stopped again as I saw the man. *I noticed that he was well fed. He was not lean or disintegrating like the rest of us. He still had the phantom of a belly pressing against his ragged shirt. His teeth were ruthless, and he showed them often, leaving his mouth perpetually hanging open to reveal the crooked and yellowed shards. His long black hair was slicked back with its own grime, left in sick curls down the back of his neck. He was enjoying this, every moment of it, and his eyes twinkled in pure sadism.*

He waited calmly for me to resurface and continue.

"He smiled and said, 'Why should you get to keep your pretty wife?' Then Dante was in front of me. I heard the shot echo as he collapsed. They just laughed as they walked away. They were the last 'people' I ever saw, besides you."

"How long before I found you?"

"Days. Maybe."

"No wonder you were such a mess," he said with levity.

"That is an understatement." I laughed as the tide of memory began to recede back under the surface.

"You good?" he asked, reaching up and pressing his palm to my cheek.

I closed my eyes and leaned into the touch just briefly. I breathed the dust in the air deep into my lungs and back out. All the flashbacks and reliving wouldn't resuscitate them. All of the memory wouldn't bring me back. There was only his hand lingering on my cheek now.

"Yes," I said, before opening my eyes.

He swept his arm under mine and guided me to my feet. He pressed a hand on both of my shoulders until he seemed assured I was stable once again. I had no secrets from him now. He knew how I failed my entire family; he knew how I quietly lusted for him. Somewhere deep down, I was sure he knew how savage I truly was. Naked, turned inside out, he saw me now.

As we marched over the dead land, the city continued to tease my peripherals. The hazy shapes of real buildings taunted me, whispered to me in the distance. Something about it, something I couldn't articulate. It was drawing me from my very center; somewhere deep inside me that didn't make sense.

I tried to ignore the sensation. I tried to focus on the way his head bobbed slightly as he walked in front of me or the way cacti still managed to bloom flowers. Yet it insisted on nagging me. My muscles itched. My clothes felt uncomfortable. My pack was trying to rip off my arms. My head started quietly to throb. We were going the wrong way. The farther we walked away from the city, the more my body began to protest. It called to me, somewhere in my bones, and it was becoming physically impossible to ignore.

"I think we need to go into that city," I said.

"What city?" he said, without looking back.

"That city, in the distance over there. The one we could see from the pass."

"I told you, cities are suicide."

"I know. We need to go into that city. I just *know* we need to go there."

"That doesn't make any sense. No." He said it shortly, immediately, with finality.

I felt a defiant flare flash over me.

"No? I'm sorry? What do I look like, your subordinate? Do I have some stupid fucking symbol Velcroed to my chest? I'm going into that city."

I turned my boots toward the figment squatting on the edge of our world. He moved quickly to step in front of me.

"Why? Why this out of nowhere? You know that is the place most likely to be crawling with them," he said.

"I don't know. I just need to. I follow you. I have always just followed you. But I need to go there."

"Pulling indirect suicide on me. Is this about your husband flashback? Xavier?"

I took a step closer to him and looked him directly in the sunglasses, seeing my own dusty, puffy eyes staring pathetically back at me. I didn't even recognize the warped reflection.

"I have wanted to die every day for months, years, whatever. Every day. Today, I just want to go into that fucking city."

"There is nothing there. It is just going to get you killed."

He looked back at me in silence, waiting for me to agree, waiting for me to follow. Step in line and march behind. Holding his eye, I sidestepped around him and headed toward the buildings jutting out of the horizon. For a moment, my own footsteps were the only sound, shuffling alone in the sand. Then I heard him trailing behind me, crunching the few shrubs. I looked back to find him just behind me and to the side.

"You are the craziest bitch I've ever known," he said.

I wasn't sure why I needed to go to the city. I could only feel my heart banging against my chest to push me that direction. I only knew if I had to trudge over any more desolate miles that looked like Dante's grave, I would find a direct way of killing myself.

And we marched on.

14

As the city grew in front of us, the buildings crumbled before our eyes. The ragged line of skyscrapers and structures I had seen, that had enticed me so deeply, dissolved into twisted shambles and skeletons of the metropolis the place once was. The city was an illusion, a mirage. Its smoking corpse was what we really found.

We entered at a distance from the vacant multilane highway with its collapsed overpasses and fractured asphalt. Cars still littered the fragmented blacktop, broken backs dangling into the fissures, doors left ajar. The fading road snaked into the fallout. The suburbs were nothing but leveled, crumbled remnants. I could make out the formulaic American city standard and the vague grid structure where cookie-cutter houses used to sit lazily; it was a confetti of domestic destruction.

"What city do you think this was?" I asked as we eased slowly over large chunks of displaced driveways and shattered siding.

"Hard to tell. Seems like the welcome sign didn't survive."

"It doesn't look like anything survived."

"If we're lucky. I think I found you in the desert east of the Rockies. New Mexico maybe? Since we crossed the pass, this could be Utah, Arizona maybe. Not like that means anything anymore."

"Surely this isn't Vegas. Uriah said it was a crater, a bomb or something."

"Definitely not Vegas. No hooker flyers. Those things would be everywhere. Plus, that would be more south. Pretty sure we would have scaled a lot more mountains."

"Fuck. Those nearly killed me. We've never been in one of the cities that got bombed before."

"There was never anything for us in them. No viable supplies, nowhere to shelter. Only the risk of attack."

"Your objections are duly fucking noted."

"As long as they're noted."

The highway led us up weathered, questionable overpasses as it slithered through what used to be. We had never followed an interstate before. We had never gone into a true city before. Dead civilization on the largest scale, miles upon miles of graveyard. I marched us toward the phantom downtown. I plainly saw it was not my glistening city, but I still had to see; I had to set my boots there.

Each step was deliberate to navigate the chaos and to keep guarded. Each time I looked over at him, he was rigid. He bounced his blade in his hand so that its shadow danced on the ground beside him. He clenched his jaw until I saw it flex in his cheek. I heard his deep and purposeful breaths. I read his body language but was inclined to ignore it. I was transfixed by what remained of the skyline.

My survivalist began to whisper to me as our safe isolation disappeared out of reach, as my nerves began to tense. What was I doing? What in the *holy fuck* was I doing? I always listened to him, always followed him. And that had kept me alive. He knew how to survive while I only knew how to tempt death. Maybe that was what I was doing. Maybe I was committing the indirect suicide he accused. Taking him with me. Eradicating the last two remaining humans. Like a good savage.

Gradually, buildings and structures began to sprout out from the desolation. First, a lone standing wall in a parking lot blown empty. Then a house with a collapsed roof. A shopping center boasting at least half its stores. Ruins emerged from rubble.

Finally, we reached what might have once been an office building. It was the tallest standing structure we had approached. From one side, it looked stable and relatively untouched. The gray concrete intersected with large lobby windows. The side of the building acted as a mirror, reflecting the nothingness behind us. Yet the other side of the building had collapsed into rubble. The entire side, all five floors, lay fragmented and crumbled in a twisted pile.

Again, we witnessed random sparing in chaotic destruction—as usual.

"I want to get a better look," I said.

"Now we're going into a half-collapsed, completely unstable structure for a better look?"

"You know, when I thought you were leading us to do something stupid, I at least kept that shit to myself."

I moved toward the building. He visibly rolled his eyes as he clomped after me. Cracks snaked over the glass of the doors and windows on the more preserved side, giving the ghastly appearance of giant spider webs, ignited by the light pouring in from the missing half of the structure. As I cautiously peeled the door back, it creaked and snapped, echoing in the empty rooms.

The destroyed office looked unnatural with sunlight pouring in, with its uniformed furniture and cubicle walls flung against the enduring structure. The tangled wreckage hunched in the shadows, hiding between what remained of the floors, partitions, and ceilings. As we eased into the daylight, it was nothing but the ragged edge where the floor simply fell away. We both stepped to the brink.

"Wow," I breathed.

"Whoa," he echoed.

Our simple one floor in elevation unfolded the devastation, the utter and complete loss of the city. My hope lay slaughtered and collapsed at my feet, my false mirage shoved in my face. The majority of the buildings were reduced to perverse structures with warped steel beams. They had been gutted, and their innards smothered the ground around them. Rubble, the entire goddamn city was nothing but wreckage and debris. How could I have seen a pardoned city here? How could I have imagined *anything* here?

We stood with our mouths agape, just staring out at a scene people had never lived to see.

The wake of utter destruction left my heart knocking hard on my ribcage. It was something my brain could barely interpret. A torrent of emotions began to swell through my extremities.

"Marcus," I said quietly.

He stopped cold and turned to stare at me. His face hung blank, stunned.

"Thank you," I said.

I had never said it. Not in all our time together. Not after the many times he had saved me.

He pushed his sunglasses up onto his forehead to look at me. I could see something brewing in the edge of his expression, something pressing against his eyes. He stepped forward. His hand found its way into my hair, and then he pulled me to him by the back of my neck. I allowed him drag me as he wanted.

His lips met my own aggressively, his face pushing hard into mine. My heart pounded already, limbs tingling, mind racing. The stubble on his face grated against my cheeks, but I didn't feel it. I opened my mouth hungrily as he started to devour me. I heard him inhale deeply as he leaned into me harder.

Finally.

I opened my mouth and felt his breath fill my lungs as his tongue slid past my teeth. My body throbbed. He wrapped around me tightly, sword bumping into my calves. I tugged him closer, arms groping at his shoulders and neck. His fingers sank in to what was left of the back of my thighs and lifted me up. I clung to his neck, pressed my chest into his, dove into his mouth. He heaved me up and slammed me against the crumbling wall as weapons clanged to the floor. His pelvis leaned into mine, and I could feel his hips through our clothes.

Our breathing collided; I could hear it ravenous and desperate. When I let my tongue tease at his earlobe, I heard him moan and felt my body flush.

Our bodies were falling into rhythm, begging for consummation, moving instinctually in a language our cells spoke fluently. I couldn't keep my eyes open; my body did not want the sensations spreading through it competing with sight. I didn't want to see anything – I wanted to *feel* every second of it.

He slid his hands up the back of my shirt. I felt his fingers on my skin, his flesh on my flesh. The warmth sent waves vibrating through me. I could feel my nerves climbing, standing on edge, stiffening and arching my body.

As I let my head fall back, as his teeth dragged slowly along my neck, I saw a figure out of the corner of my eye.

"You've got to be fucking kidding me," I breathed.

They were on him first, before either of us really knew what was coming, lost in each other. They ripped him back, and I fell hard onto the concrete floor. I saw his body topple off the edge of the floor and vanish from view as I struggled to collect myself.

They watched him fall then turned to me, circling and panting, as I slid back up the wall. That wretched, primal sound. Pain radiated up my back as impact echoed in my muscles. I gathered his sword in one hand and my cutlass in the other as they eased toward me, eyes wide, mouths wagging, fingers wriggling.

They all looked the same to me now.

These two had the same filthy skin, the same bulging eyes and disgusting, murderous look on their faces. It had once been terrifying and unnerving to see what I knew to have once been people so lowered and living decayed; yet now, even in the peril of this moment, I just wanted to roll my eyes at the monotony of them all. They had devolved out of individuality, out of personality, which I had never realized were hallmarks of humanity. Animals were fucking boring.

I recognized the black utility belt clinging to the melted waist of one. He had been a cop. The cuffs, the gun, the pepper spray all long ago stripped, leaving the pockets unsnapped and flapping. His tattered clothes were the right dark blue to have been a uniform once upon a past lifetime. He let his mouth hang open as saliva streamed from one corner and pooled down his chest. My heart sank a little lower as I pictured Dante donning his uniform for his graduation, how he puffed up a little straighter and strutted across the bedroom to the door, how he couldn't stop smiling under that ridiculous hat.

The other toddled as a skeleton with only a thin layer of stretched flesh enveloping her. I could barely make out her deflated breasts from her protruding ribs. When she stretched her fingers toward me, I saw the tendons shift up her forearm; I saw her bicep ripple sickly. Open sores covered her gray skin, red and brown craters in what remained of her, windows practically to her bones. I wondered if these two had been married, if they had managed to fall together. I wondered if they would even remember what they had been to each other.

In that moment, I saw my boys—Dante, Jordi, Eli—waiting for me. *Dante wore his faded Bears shirt, hair and goatee clipped short and clean. Jordi stood beside him, standing on his toes, reaching as high as he could to wave to me. He smiled wide, so excited it might spill off his cheeks. Dante had one hand on Jordi's bouncing shoulder and had Eli wrapped up in the other arm. Eli was his perfect shade of caramel, not* green. *He grinned a broad, childish grin that exposed his lone two teeth jutting out from his lower gums. They all smiled at me; they were all welcoming me.* I knew this was the moment. I could lay down the fight and finally join them; I could give the fuck up, and it could finally just be over. For both of us.

Free. Forgiven.

I knew Marcus was alive below where I stood, on the other side of these two hollow savages.

His shadow against the sky as I looked over the three dead bodies, sword outstretched, gun at his thigh.

His breath on my neck as he restrained me in the desert.

The smile spread across his face as he itemized the bug out bags in the prepper house and packed his bag heavier.

Xavier sleeping on his thigh by the firelight.

The sword in his hand draped over the two of us as we slept huddled together on the ground.

His hands in the dirt and his lips lingering on Xavier's cold skin.

His hand laced in mine as we co-slept with a grave.

The smell of his dirty skin as I pressed my face against him for warmth.

The sound of his footsteps following me into this death trap.

They stepped closer still. My heart pounded as my survivalist seized back control of my cognitive functions.

I tightened my grip on our worn weapons and lifted them high.

15

I dismembered them together, mingling their bloody pieces in an indistinguishable pile. If they had once been a couple, they would not be able to be separated now. Death could reunite their parts. With the echoes of their panting and shrieks fading from the building, my survivalist abandoned me, and my mind fell back into my head.

"Marcus," I breathed.

I found him crawling where the collapsed floor met the dirt. He leaned to the side, bracing himself along the rubble with a twisted piece of rebar clutched in his fist. Another couple of bodies lay crumpled behind him. Blood painted the dusty chunks as I counted the two bludgeoned heads. He cradled his ribs and stepped cautiously until he heard me jumping and sliding to him.

"Neutralized?" he panted.

I nodded. "In pieces. No sign of others. Yet."

He stopped and pressed his back into a large piece of concrete with rebar snaking out of the edges like industrial weeds. I scuffled down a long angle of misplaced floor and landed beside him. The impact of my boots kicked up tiny clouds of dirt. I stood in front of him and leaned forward, running my hands along his neck and opening his coat to inspect him. A wound on his forehead spewed a trail of blood down the side of his face, mingling and converging with sweat. Yet no protruding bones, no gaping holes. He looked good enough to move. Without additional thought, without question, I swooped under his wounded side and propped him up against me.

I felt the weight of his side against my shoulder as I forced my steps to guide us straight, the most direct path out of this mistake. I could hear him wincing and tightening his breathing in my ear. I didn't care if it was exposed, I didn't care if we had just killed four savages—the highway was the quickest route back to safety. I dragged him back onto the fractured and faded asphalt, back over the questionable overpasses, back through the lack of suburbia until we could see the desert spreading out in front of us again.

The outside of my calf and the depths of my thigh began to whine and burn in the exertion of walking for both of us, but his breathing began to calm the farther we hobbled. I felt him reclaim more and more of his own weight. Finally, he wobbled upright and let his arm slip from around my shoulders. He stopped for a moment and attempted to straighten his torso, only to collapse back into a hunched and protected position. He adjusted his pack, shifting the weight to the undamaged side, and started moving.

As the city dissolved behind us, he stood on his own again. He hobbled awkwardly, limped with a wide stance.

"Are you hit?" I asked, turning my head at him. "More than your side?"

"No." He sort of laughed. "First time I've ever had to fight with blue balls. Yep, pretty awful. Walking it off, just walking it off. Let's get the fuck out of here."

He adjusted himself. Then readjusted himself again, protectively clutching his ribs as he did. I probably shouldn't have smiled, but I did. A genuine smile that I felt in my chest. In another life, I would have blushed.

"I think I'll go back to letting you lead," I said when it was far enough away to be safe to laugh.

"You're goddamn right you will. You suck at it. You are an awful battle buddy."

"What is a battle buddy?"

"The guy to your right, the guy watching your back when you're in the shit."

"One horrible decision and I'm an awful battle buddy?"

"Today, yes. Redo tomorrow. Maybe." He was slowly starting to walk normally, only hunched toward his wounded side. "Everyone knows there's a special bond between brothers in arms. Smitty was my battle buddy. And yes, we had the ridiculous call signs like Razor."

"What was yours?"

"Razor."

I laughed out loud at him. We could have been mistaken for a couple leaving a movie. If we weren't covered in blood. This could have been mistaken for a date. If we weren't combat drunk.

"I saved his ass, he saved my ass," he continued. "But Smitty and I were close. Closer than we should have been. Don't look at me like that. Not any *Brokeback Mountain* shit, though that was known to happen. Don't ask, don't tell. We swore if we made it out, every year we would go fishing or camping or whatever the fuck. He kept me alive in the darkest, and I don't even know how he died when all this happened."

We didn't know what had happened to most of them. My parents in Indiana. The two women I ate lunch with every day at work. Jordi and Eli's teachers. Our next-door neighbor with the yapping dog that never shut up. The high school boy who bagged my groceries. The mindless drones on the treadmills after work. The boys in Dante's precinct. It was inconceivable just how many people, how many strings and connections tangled up in our lives, were instantly severed. They were all dead; this was something we *knew* without needing proof, but how they died was both a mystery and irrelevant. Tragic explanations would only lay more wounds upon the already scarred backs of the survivors. It was better not to know - it was better to forget they ever existed at all.

He winced and forced hard breaths through strained lips as I helped him ease down to the ground.

"I think it's just some cracked ribs," he said, "nothing to really worry about."

"Take off your shirt."

"Hey now. I'm not that easy."

"Obviously. I let you do the killing and training. Let me do what I do."

"What do you do?"

"I was a nurse," I paused. "Let me rephrase. I started nursing school. Then sold out."

"How did I not know this?"

"Never came up."

I let my fingers wander over the ripple of his ribs. His breathing stumbled and his side tightened. When my fingers landed on a soft pocket of blooming fluid, he visibly flinched and cried out through his teeth. I pressed my ear to his warm chest and listened to the steady thump of his heartbeat and the air moving in his lungs. I let my hand linger at his side, savoring the simple feeling of his skin as I leaned back up.

"Yeah, I think it's just broken ribs. Nothing sounds punctured. You are lucky as fuck."

He smiled. "I told you we were the lucky ones."

"Yeah, yeah. Now shut it. You need to rest. I'll deal with the fire, the food. You just fucking lay there. And shut it."

"So this nurse business…"

"That's not shutting it."

"What do you mean you sold out?"

I gathered the few sticks and shrubs nearby as he refused to shut it. I dug through our sacks for the flint and more cans of prepper food.

"I mean I sold out. I started, and—I don't know— it was too competitive or too long. I didn't want to change adult diapers. I met Dante, and I just wanted to get there, you know? Get married, get settled, have kids. I just fell into the medical billing bullshit. A job I hated that paid the bills so I could live the personal life I wanted."

"I know how that goes. I just enlisted for the college money. Never thought we would be at war so long. Never thought I would get stop-lossed more than once. Just tried to suffer through to get to that magic place."

"In the end, it doesn't get better, it just keeps going. We are granted seconds of perfect happiness, and we never notice them because we are too busy fixating on getting 'there'. There is no there. We only get *now*." All those moments I took for granted. All the times I got spun up over stupid shit. "Dante's father used to say, 'Sometimes you have to enjoy the ride to the bottom because that's all you have.' I don't think I ever appreciated what that meant until now, until it was really all just gone."

"That's the bitch of it, isn't it? Nothing new. We never figure it out until it's too fucking late."

"Apparently. Now I just have regrets."

"Survivors always do."

He wrapped his arms tighter around himself and shuttered a bit. I walked around the small fire and crouched down beside him, putting my hand to his face. I pressed the back of my hand to his forehead, then my palm to his cheek.

"You're warm," I said.

"I'm fine."

"Probably your body just reacting to the trauma. That was one hell of a fall. I wasn't sure if I was going to lose you, too."

"Not that easy, Parker."

I smiled and settled down beside him, handing him a can of baked beans.

"Beans? You must really be feeling guilty."

"Shut it."

I woke up in the morning not cold but nestled against him just the same. His arm encircled my waist, sword still held fast at the end. I peered up at his sleeping face and let my fingertips gently find his forehead. Cool again. The fever had passed in the night. He would not turn green before my eyes and seize his way into my last grave.

I shifted to sit up, yet he restrained me down with him.

"Where are you going?" he mumbled, eyes still closed.

"Just to piss."

I moved to stand again, and he continued to hold me, but I could hear the hesitance in his breathing.

"Don't strain yourself, now," I said, taking his arm and placing it at his side. "You'll be worthless to me." The remains of the city were far enough behind us now. Again, it appeared as the illusion of a skyline in the distance. This far away, I could not make out the damage. It was just promising shapes teasing the space with possibility.

"I think we should camp here a couple days," I said, "let you recover a bit."

"We never camp more than one night."

"I know, but you also never had cracked ribs."

"We don't know this area."

"We haven't known any of these areas."

"We need to continue west."

"West? What's with you and west? What do you think is out there?"

"Do you know how you felt about that city? Like you just had to go, had to see. That's how I feel about going west."

"Yeah and look how that turned out."

"We have to try. I have to know."

"Fine. We'll go west. Only if we rest for a day or two."

"Westward, ho," he smiled.

16

For an unprecedented day, we camped. We did not flee by the smoke of dying embers in the fire. We did not march. He laid his head on my leg and napped as I lounged against a large rock. And just sat. It felt as if I had not sat down since the first news report flickered across our living room.

Dante held a cookie suspended in front of his mouth, milk dripping back into the glass in his hand. Jordi galloped on his knees as he guided a toy monster truck over the unruly terrain of the carpet. Eli tried to swim on his belly across the floor, planting his face down and shrieking when his muscles failed to comply. I let the magazine slip from my fingers and tumble into a pile at my feet as horror started infiltrating our home.

Marcus did insist that we could not simply curl up and nap together, one of us had to remain somewhat vigilant. I doubted we would see many here, in the fallen-out desert stretching out from a crater of a city. Not enough resources to stay and survive, even for the uncivilized and savage. But if they were teeming around what was left of Vegas—if anything Uriah had uttered was to be believed—we couldn't take the risk of fully letting our guard down.

That mistake had just nearly gotten us killed already.

I let my hand rest gently near his injured ribs, which had started to show purple on his skin overnight, perpetually gauging his breathing. I felt his side inflate up against his soiled shirt and tell me what I needed to know. He was still flinching and hobbling around, though he tried to disguise it from me. There was no mistaking the lack of upright rigidity in his stance.

I had never watched him sleep before. He always waited me out, until exhaustion pulled me under, or hid under the dark veil of the night between us. Even beneath his sunglasses, I could see the expressions surfacing on his face. His cheeks and mouth twitched in his dreams. Was he seeing our savagery? Was he still seeing Iraq? Was he seeing *her*? There was an ample menu of traumas from which to choose.

The stubble had run rampant on his face since the last time he had hacked it back with his freshly sharpened knife. An entire lifetime had sprung up to distract him. More had happened since that fateful moment in prepper hell than in all the time since the world fell. Dirt traced out the wrinkles gradually wearing into his face. I wondered what he had looked like crisp, clean, and crew cut in the last life.

As he dozed, I leaned back and allowed my mind the rare permission to wander. I thought of him lifting me up and slamming me into that forgotten office wall. I felt the reciprocity in my desire; I felt the anxious relief in his hands. He had wanted me, too. I thought about him following me into that fallen out city. He had known what we would find; he had known what I was risking. Yet he pursued me anyway, protected me in my ignorance. I thought about catching up to his broken form outside the building, smited for my stupidity. The enormity of the fact that, for all the times he saved me, I nearly got him killed bloomed heavily on my chest. I reached down and let my hand rest on his head.

Now, it was not that I wanted him. Now it was that I loved him.

"It's creepy to watch someone sleep, you know," he mumbled from my lap.

"You're supposed to be resting."

"What does it look like I'm doing?"

"Talking shit."

"I can do that and rest."

"How are the ribs?"

"I'm fine."

"Okay. Now seriously, how are the ribs?" I started to softly press my hand against his side. He grunted and shifted.

"Little tender still."

"Maybe we should camp another day."

"No. We can't. Today is enough of a risk. Back at it at dawn."

The sun steadily climbed the sky over us, perpetually reducing our oasis of shade. It warmed my boots first, spreading heat over toes wriggling in filmy socks. I could feel the warmth rising from the dirt around us, throbbing in the air. I had never cared for the desert, in this life or the last. I had never seen the beauty in desolation. I could only be thankful that it was not summer.

It was strange to do nothing after an endless blur of relentless activity—walking, fighting, searching, mourning. My body told me it had been years in the faded way it failed to even resemble its former form, in the perpetual cries of the depleted and strained muscles. My heart told me it had been yesterday and decades simultaneously, both too close and too far from all I had lost.

As we basked in foreign laziness, in the distance, we heard a shift in the sand, a scuff against a rock. Not the randomness of nature, something deliberate. He snapped up then silently faltered, grimacing as he cradled his ribs.

I snatched up his sword before he could reach for it and crawled beside him, angrily signaling for him to lie back down. I knew he was glaring at me from behind his lenses as he reluctantly complied. I clutched his sword and eased around the rock.

Just once, let it be a fucking deer.

I pressed my back against the rock as I raised the sword to the ready. My heart pounded in my chest, priming my body and my muscles for the fight. I took a calming breath and mentally shoved aside all thoughts. I brought my brain to focus and swung around to look over the rock.

It was a fucking deer.

The large mule deer glimpsed me as I saw him. We both froze, locked in a cautious stare. He brought his neck up slowly, holding my gaze, until his antlers reached into the sky above him. I let the sword gently lower in front of me, still in my grip, still prepared. A long, silent moment wafted between us. We did not move, we did not breathe. We both studied each other and waited. The sun dug into the knobs of his antlers and cast grotesque shadows against the sand. I could hear the animal's heartbeat, I could feel his heat. I felt myself surge in the presence of one living thing that did not want to kill me.

And I did not want to kill him.

I let a long, slow breath spill out of my lips. The deer blinked and jerked its neck. Then, in an instant, he leapt over the nearest rock and bounded across the sand. I lowered the sword to my side as I watched him go, kicking up sand with each graceful leap. Without a strike, I eased back to the ground and guided Marcus back to my lap.

"So a medical claims billing specialist and a cop. How did that happen?" he said, randomly piercing our silence.

"In a bar. Where most things in my young life happened. When I was in school and he was in the academy."

"And you just said, 'Fuck it. I don't want to be a nurse anymore'?"

"I just loved him. He was all I wanted. I forgot about wanting other things for myself."

"Sounds healthy. How'd that work out for you?"

"He wasn't a piece of shit, so not bad. I still loved him, loved our family. Just not my job. Happens when you sell out. Let me guess. Was your wife a stripper true to her name, right off the base?"

"No," he huffed. "She was a cocktail waitress at a strip club right off the base. But not for long after I met her."

The memory was rising in me. I couldn't fight it off. Even having him in my lap, talking about his wife cocktailing in a strip club, could not dissuade the ghosts.

The pub seethed as a mass of bodies, pulsating and moving as one organism. Above the dull roar of drunken chatter, I heard drink splash and meet its demise on the floor, no doubt all over more than one person. An inebriated woman cackled in my ear before nearly swiping across my face to playfully slap her date's shoulder. The sea of people foamed in green. Not one body was unadorned by the color. Shamrocks plagued the scene. I kept my elbows tucked in and my dark pint of beer against my chest as I shimmied and slunk through the wobbling crowd. Until a sharp impact sent me lurching forward and my precious drink colliding with the floor.

"You stupid bitch," I muttered as I brushed off my hands and turned to face the asshole who had nearly knocked me off my feet.

Dante's young face met me with a wide, white smile splitting his dark cheeks. I felt the anger evaporate out of the back of my skull.

"I'm so sorry," he said, stepping closer to me. I felt the air between us charge. "Let me buy you a new beer."

A single tear rolled from my cheek and splashed down on the lens of his sunglasses.

"Peace time is treacherous," he said from my lap. "It's easy to stay distracted, stay on mission with your head in the fight. But when it gets quiet, when you have the time to think about all you've seen and all you've done, that's when all the noncombat events run rampant. The suicides, the 'accidental discharges' in each other's heads. Without an enemy, we turn on ourselves."

"You ever turn?"

"A little. Nothing too serious. I did the normal, stupid shit. Smoked like a chimney, pounded energy drinks until my heart might explode, hauled ass in vehicles. Small rebellious acts of self-destruction, trying to convince myself I controlled my life and my death. Not the IEDs on the ground or the mortars in the air. I always got low in down time. I thought about her, compared the man she married to the sad son of a bitch who would leave Iraq. If I was that lucky. Smitty always made sure to pull me out of it, though. Another reason you always need a good battle buddy."

"Unless they get you thrown off a building."

"Unless they get you thrown off a building."

I smiled at the levity of it, but guilt hung on the corners of my mouth, pulled down on my features. The sensation weighed my shoulders, heavied my head. I could not shake or ignore that I had nearly gotten him killed. After everything he had managed to survive.

"Was there anything worth seeing in Iraq?" I asked.

"Iraq was a shit hole. Smelled like shit and fireworks. They burned their trash and their shit. If you fell into a canal, you had to get like a hundred shots. Rats' nest of an electrical system that never stayed up in the heat and that electrocuted gunners left and right. I would never choose to go back, if it's even still there, but there's always something to see."

"Like?"

"Sunsets. There was so much sand and dirt in the air that it would literally rain mud, but it would also create these crazy colored sunsets. Sun looked like it was on fire, clouds shifted between so many different colors. And the oil refineries burning off at night while I was looking out the window of a Blackhawk. The city lights were a mix of electric and actual fire, depending on the part of Baghdad. Then there were these stacks at the refineries, burning above the rest like huge candles."

"A little girl sitting next to an IED?"

"Yeah. In a weird, saved-my-ass sort of way - that might have been the most beautiful thing I saw."

He paused for a moment. I had no doubt he saw her little visage in front of him right now, sand-streaked and windblown. She haunted me, and I had never laid eyes on her at all.

"What was the best thing about having kids?" He shifted the subject.

"That's a painful question."

"Aren't they all now? Don't worry, the answer will hurt me as much as it hurts you."

I didn't want to think about it. I didn't want to remember one good thing, though my mind was always brimming with the memories of all I buried. My past life was a swollen flood waiting for the smallest leak to surge into my present. It wanted to pour over and drown me. As much as I would have happily suffocated to feel any of those moments once more, my survivalist went to great lengths to keep it locked back, bound and gagged in the black corner of my tortured brain. I was its victim, and it was mine. I choked on the question for a moment longer, while the survivor in me battled back the gaping emotional vacancy in my heart, then I breathed slowly before I could look back without being consumed.

"I could say *everything*, but that wouldn't be true. Everyone always says everything. But it's not; a lot of it is hard, and a lot of it sucks. There are these moments where you think, what the fuck have I done? The best part is that they're totally worth it, that you would go through all the pain again for them even knowing it was coming. You love them so much it completes your life and breaks your heart at the same time. They show you what it's like to be amazed by the world again."

"Yep." He closed his eyes and pressed his head back against my thigh. "Hurt like hell."

"Tell me about it. You would have been a good father, though, Marcus."

"Don't say that," he breathed. "I would have gotten it killed."

"You can't say that. You can't know that."

"I got Xavier killed. What more is there to know?"

"No, you didn't. They killed him. I failed to protect him on my own fucking chest."

"I led you in killing his parents. I led Uriah into our camp and led them to us. I killed him."

"It's not that simple. Did I get my babies and my husband killed? Was there really any way we could have protected them in a world like this?"

He did not respond. I knew he did not want to hear what I had said. No words from my lips could dissuade him from persecuting and blaming himself. He was briefly falling away from me in my own lap, abandoning his body to not deal with it. I felt his head grow heavier as he stared up at the sky past me. I did not waste anymore words – I simply waited.

"Why do you ask me about Iraq all the time?" he finally asked.

"I don't know. Curious, I guess."

In my life, I had seen two worlds—my one before and this one now. He had seen somewhere different before the fall. It was something unfathomable to me, and like all things foreign and mysterious, it quietly beckoned my interest. It was not here now, and it was not then that solicited my suicide. It was just a dream in someone else's memories. It was somewhere else.

"People were always curious," he said. "Wanted to know all the gory details. How many people did you kill? Did you see anyone die? It sounds like you consider it the savagery baseline, some kind of proof for how you think."

"Wouldn't that be what war is?"

"Not that simple. Especially in this effects-based, non-kinetic wartime approach."

"I have no idea what you just said."

"Neither do I."

He laughed softly. We let the conversation blow across the desert day. The sun softly cooked me, enticing sweat across my skin. I would have shed some layers, but I did not want to jostle him. For once, I felt at peace in the quiet, the silence seemed comfortable. With so much of his mind poured out between us, he was no longer a mocking enigma. With our bodies touching, he was no longer forbidden. I let him wallow in my lap for a few lazy moments; then I had to ask.

It was time to know.

"Since we're just sitting here, putting it all out there, can I ask you something?" I finally said.

"Sure." He kept his eyes closed, warming in the sun like a lizard.

"Why did you save me? I get your whole moral code thing, but you never saw anyone else who needed help?"

"You know, by that point, most were past help. In one way or another. But no. It was you. Something about you. I had seen that look of surrender and defeat, that invitation to death a thousand fucking times in too many places. They had all just given up—just died or turned without a fight. I couldn't stand it again."

Something in me. What could there have possibly been in me? I was nothing but failure and a solicitation for death. I was an empty shell, a hollow corpse. There was nothing in me that day.

"And why did you keep me? Train me? Save me over and over?"

"I told you before – when you save a life, you're responsible for it."

"That seems a little backwards. Shouldn't I owe you for saving me?"

"No. Saving you did enough. I would have cracked up as the only one all this time. Uriah would have eaten my ass or something."

"And the battle buddy is redeemed."

"My ribs still hurt like hell. Let's call it breaking even."

Without another word, he took my hand and interlaced it with his. Then he set the entanglement of digits calmly on his chest. His heartbeat thumped faintly against my skin. Those forgotten nerves webbing my hand together sang out in tactile memory.

"Mommy! Mommy! Hold hands!" How the small hand wrapped around my index finger. Dante's fingers parting mine and digging into the top of my hand as he

clutched me close and thrust into me. "I love you... I love you..."

I closed my eyes to try to keep another tear from plummeting onto his face. I pushed the air out of my lungs methodically until Dante's voice was no longer in my ears. Then I looked out and let myself feel Marcus's hand against mine again. I permitted it to feel good and reassuring.

As I stared out in front of me, Amber Lynn materialized out of the heat wavering in the air. Her long blonde hair twirled in wind that wasn't blowing. She rubbed her hand over a bump that was never given the time to grow. Dante clawed up and unearthed himself from the sand under which I had hastily and sloppily buried him. The dirt fell away and vanished from him as he stood.

They didn't shamble like the dead; they didn't walk like the living. They were just beside us, all around us. Amber Lynn appeared on one side of us and slowly and gently lowered herself to a seat on the ground. Dante squatted quickly, letting himself drop to the other side of us. They crouched down, got comfortable, settled in for a front row seat. Close enough to breathe on us, if they were breathing.

Amber Lynn wrapped her arms protectively around her imagined belly and looked forlornly at his head so comfortable on my thigh. She reached forward to touch his face then retracted, replaced her palm on her stomach. Dante dug his elbows into his knees, pressed his chin heavy on balled up fists. He stared at our hands wound together. I turned my head sideways and leaned toward him, but he only fixated on where my fingers tangled Marcus.

Behind them, a sea of memories from our entire past lives swelled high enough to blot out the sun.

Marcus stirred to sit up. I pressed my hands into his back to help guide him. Amber Lynn and Dante stood and parted, moved to allow him to stand. As Marcus hobbled awkwardly around the rock, Amber Lynn trailed him, her blonde hair waving like a flag behind her. Dante remained with me but refused to look at me. With Marcus out of sight, I moved in front of Dante, begged his eyes. He simply continued to stare down at my hands in my lap and slightly rock from side to side. I pressed my hand to my mouth in an attempt not to cry.

Marcus appeared and half-smiled at me as he ran his hand along the side of the rock for support. Amber Lynn continued to haunt his steps. She closed her eyes as she inhaled at the back of his neck. He did not see her; he did not feel her. He was alone in the camp with me while I was crowded by our dead. I turned away from Dante and stood, rubbing the impression Marcus' head had left in my leg.

"Hungry?" I asked.

He nodded as he eased back down to the ground, folding his hands behind his head. Amber Lynn encircled her arms protectively around her belly again. She knelt down beside him gracefully, staring at his face wide eyed now that he was not using me as a pillow, not touching me. She only took a second to shoot me a look from the sharp corner of her blue eye.

I breathed and tried to ignore the bitchy figment, moving to our packs. Dante trailed me then stepped to place one foot on either side of Marcus's bag. As I unzipped the backpack between his legs, Dante crossed his arms and shifted side to side as he always did when he was growing impatient. I looked up at him and tried to snag his eye contact. *Just look at me already*.

"What are you looking at?" Marcus asked.

"Nothing," I mumbled.

I buried my face back in the pack. I retrieved dehydrated meals and set the two packages on the ground beside me to fish for his canteen.

"Eating fancy tonight," he commented.

"Well, it is a vacation day."

He chuckled. Amber Lynn looked over to roll her eyes at me. Dante did not react. Our camp suddenly felt overpopulated.

As I crouched down to prepare the meals, Dante stooped down behind me. I tried to pretend he wasn't there because I knew he truly was not. Yet somehow, I felt his breath on the back of my neck, I felt the heat radiating from his body. I closed my eyes tight, knowing he was cold and breathless in another desert. I felt his hand rise and slide down the center of my back. His familiar combination to my body, the firm pressure sending waves through my nerves. I tried not to gasp, fought not to jerk. When his fingers abandoned me, I finished collecting dinner and ate surrounded by ghosts. I did not even taste the food.

That night, as the sun died in the sky, Marcus pulled me close to him in the dirt. The dark tugged a cold blanket over the desert and left the air feeling thin in my lungs. He draped himself around my back, nestled his chin in my shoulder. We pulled the ratty blanket around us. I huddled and shuttered until his body heat spread to me. Exhaustion began to flirt with me, I could feel it pressing on my forehead.

Dante shifted in the growing darkness and lay down beside me. He arranged himself right alongside us, looking into my eyes as he always did when we went to bed, looking into my eyes for the first time since he had appeared. With that familiar drowsy affection on his face, he took my hand and closed his eyes. The weight of his hand was comforting as it guided me over into sleep's waiting arms.

I never saw him again.

17

Time became a mirage in the desert, as it always had. As it had when Dante and I stumbled through our blinding grief, as it had when I sought death from three random savages, as it had when he scooped me up from the bloody dirt and began reshaping me. Once we put our feet to trudging again, it dissolved into a blur of walking and sleeping. We took to moving in the dusk and dawn hours, when we could still see but suffer the piercing sun less.

By gradual degrees, he healed. His entire side was no longer a nauseating purple, so deep the flesh looked swollen and dead. Green and yellow permeated the bruise and started to make it look like living tissue again. His breath still caught in a noiseless grunt when he moved. For days, I carried his pack like a large pregnant belly, waddling as the two bags neutralized each other, pulling me in both directions. He had resisted, puffed up and insisted he could carry on, but he could not camouflage or deny such a contusion.

Oh, the irony of forcing him to rest after I had just wanted him to fuck me for so long.

As we slept each afternoon, huddled in shrinking shade, I lay on my back and pulled him onto my chest, serving as his pillow, offering whatever comfort for the ribs I had broken.

At one point, it felt like the desert would sprawl out in front of us forever. Windswept sand in every direction. Entire forgotten cities could be beneath our boots. I imagined our footsteps falling above Phoenix, Reno, Salt Lake, any of the desert cities I had never seen. Who knew if we were in Arizona, Utah, Nevada, California? I was horrendous at geography even when there was geography to know. All that mattered anymore was west. *Westward, ho.* Who knew if there was anything left after this desert? Who knew if this desert would simply drop off into the ocean? It would be fitting to just perish here, where I ended and where we began.

Then I saw it in the distance, tall and lonely, thin leaves wavering high in the plain sky. The first palm tree. The first promise of another destination, the first breadcrumb to flee to the next climate. It staked its claim against the desolation, and other vegetation slowly began to amass support behind it. The world changed beneath our feet, one step at a time, until the desert faded away into yet another plaguing memory.

"Is it weird that we haven't seen anything?" I said as we meandered down a gentle slope.

"Seen any what?"

"Any anything. No savages, no nothing."

"Maybe. Can't be too surprised in the desert, you know."

"True enough. So we should watch for more now."

"The greener it gets."

"Will we ever really outrun them?"

"Maybe," he said again. "That's the idea. Find where they end. Find where there is something else."

"I hope you're right."

"Me, too."

I could taste the salt starting to taint the air. I could feel it creeping into my lungs and giving each breath flavor. I knew the feel of the approaching sea, felt its pull. The fluttering sensation in my chest reminded me of my own childhood, my own small hand hidden in my father's as he guided me along the beach for the first time and I met the big blue beast that looked large enough to swallow me whole. Something both awe-inspiring and terrifying captivating me.

We heard it first; the distant, steady frothing of the waves, but after summiting the right hill, the flat blue horizon finally betrayed the land. The water stretched out so far it bent the sky, curved the world. The angry introduction of waves breaking upon the shore stretched out into tranquility, water that appeared flat enough to walk on. It was the light at the end of a long and horrendous tunnel paved with only graves. Deep in the pit of my stomach, I did not care if that light was buried suffocating, deep beneath the waves.

Whatever made it end.

I had tunnel vision. I did not see the slopes we continued down. I did not notice when foliage forfeited to sand. I felt an exhilaration rising in me as the ocean ahead of us consumed more and more of my sight, became more ominous and real. Whether a pack of savages, a watery grave, or nothing at all greeted us at the shoreline, it would finally be something different. There would be nowhere left to walk or wander, no direction left to explore. One way or another, this would finally be the end. While I felt a pessimistic pressure on my heart, I also swelled with relief. I would let it swallow me whole.

We finally arrived at the end of our world. Our footsteps sank deep into the sand, different from any desert. Our pace faltered, mired in a new terrain and in awe of the foreground. The sea was all that lay ahead of us. It danced in undulating surf, spoke in the primal lashing tongue of the waves, breathed in the sea gusts against our faces. Finally standing on its precipice, it looked like isolation. This immeasurable monster sprawled out endlessly between us and anything else. We were stranded on our continent with no idea about the rest of the wide world, like the natives generations ago. I stared blankly at the broken-backed ships forever rocking on the shore.

It was over. Where would we go now?

I stood watching the spray silently for a long time, letting the sea air tangle my hair, letting the salt water my eyes. I could not discern how I felt. My emotions rolled in my chest to mirror the rocking body of water in which I presently lost my mind. I breathed slow and heavy before finally turning to him.

He had dropped to the sand beside me. His pack was already stripped from his back and resting on the ground. He slowly contorted himself until he could strip the boots from his feet. He left them arranged on the sand beside the bag, socks stuffed safely within. He eased himself up and began walking barefoot toward the water. Then he stopped at the wet edge of the sand and looked back at me, waited for me. Confused and hesitant, I followed his lead, shed my worn boots, then took tentative, unprotected steps after him. He stretched out his hand and hooked his fingers around mine as we walked toward the sea.

The wet sand felt different than the dry. It had no heat. It held together and fought more convincingly against our weight. My feet had felt nothing but the inside of my boots for too long. The nerves were baffled by the free air, tantalized by the sandy massage. A small wave collapsed in front of us and raced out thin and fast over the sand. The water met my toes as my skin shrieked happily. He kept my hand in his as we submitted our legs to the ocean, as we felt the tide swell up around our calves and soak the bottoms of our pant legs.

When the surf played at our knees, he finally stopped his slow march. I looked over at him. I did not recognize his face. He had pushed his sunglasses onto his head, and his eyes squinted against the light bouncing off the ocean. His mouth and nose scrunched up. His other hand played at his chin. He was shifting, moving in unfamiliar ways. Then he let out a long breath, and the chuckle began to pour out of his thin lips.

"Are you laughing?" I asked incredulously, the movement of the sea causing me to sway.

"What else is there to do?"

He met my eyes uncomposed, raw. His face moved loose as so many expressions painted over it. I reached up and pressed my palm to his stubbled cheek. He half-smiled and kept shifting back and forth until I dropped my arm back to my side. I retrieved my hand from his, sighed, and let my eyes wander off into the bobbing distance. All these miles, all these years; to be standing knee deep in the pitching ocean, listening to the shattered hulls of floundering vessels ever smashing against the shore.

"What are we going to do now?" I said.

He stopped moving. He fell still, only shifted by the will of the sea, and I could hear him breathing deliberately over the roar of the surf. He was thinking, wrestling within his own brain. I saw the contest shift in his brow, in the clenching of his forearms as he moved his hands. I stood beside him and waited. He gazed out upon the waves for a long time, long enough for me to question if he ever intended on answering me. Then he snapped out of it. He turned and looked me so dead and hard in the eyes that I felt my chest flinch.

"Well, that's settled," he said softly. "We've looked. I've dragged you all over this country looking for survivors, *real* survivors. We both know how that went. There is no one here. All I brought us was more death, more pain. I led us here, through all this shit. Now I'll let you decide. We can go back, go up into the mountains, find some place remote enough, and live. Stop moving like I know you've wanted. Or we can take to the water, keep looking, find out if the whole world is like this."

His words left my mouth agape. Had he just forfeited the fight? Had he just said we could settle? Had he just left the decision to me? None of this aligned with anything I expected to find when we reached the sea. I thought of Xavier plucked from a filthy closet and placed into the ground. I thought of Uriah and the other Z-branded savages rotting in appropriate pieces. I thought of the crucified sacrifices in the haunted town. I thought of Marcus plummeting off the edge of a half-collapsed building. I thought of the mirage of the city and bombed out appearance of my mistake. I thought of the red dirt in the desert congealing in my tears and my blood as I waited to die. I thought of Marcus crouching down to gather me up and set my boots on this path. I felt every single step to this moment in each cell of my body. Every tear, every drop of blood, every price so painfully paid. My head throbbed; my heart pounded. He stepped forward and guided me into his chest.

With his heartbeat in my ear, I pictured us in a cabin in the mountains. The Rockies. I knew that is where he would go, back to his motherland. I had never been into the heart of the Rockies, but I pictured the purple mountain majesty all around. I saw snowcapped peaks and furry pine trees. I envisioned the small cabin he would meticulously construct for us hidden away. We would be miles above and away from any remains of society. He would find a spot that took treachery to climb to, that was easily fortified, that had a defensive vantage point. We would dig into the dirt and pummel it until it was viable, planting a garden and crops, working the land together. Our bug out bags would be fully stocked and stashed in a corner out of sight. He would look foreign without that growth on his back, his hands would look empty without a sword in them. He would look at me and see only me. Maybe a child would toddle between us. Secluded and safe.

The vision was pleasant. As amiable and inviting as all the happy memories that threatened to kill me. That wasn't us – that wasn't this life.

Could he really live not knowing? Could we live as the last two real people on Earth? Would we ever be granted such a fantasy in this savage world?

I bit down into my lip and closed my eyes. I wanted it. I wanted that life as much as I wanted the one I had lost. I pressed the top of my skull against his chest and softly shook my head. I couldn't have the past or the future, neither existed anymore. My body tensed in conflict, my breathing restricted. Tears threatened my eyes, but he kept his hands calmly on my shoulders. I focused on his touch, on him and this odd marine moment. I concentrated on the shape of his chest against my forehead and controlled my breathing. Then I skidded my face up his shirt and turned my eyes to his. I pressed myself into him and rested my chin on his collarbone.

"Tell me about this boat idea," I said into his neck.

We stared out at the sea, he and I, as it bobbed out onto the horizon and spilled into seeming infinity.

Savages

About the Author

Colorado-bred writer, Christina Bergling knew she wanted to be an author in fourth grade.

In college, she pursued a professional writing degree and started publishing small scale. It all began with "How to Kill Yourself Slowly."

With the realities of paying bills, she started working as a technical writer and document manager, traveling to Iraq as a contractor and eventually becoming a trainer and software developer.

She avidly hosted multiple blogs on Iraq, bipolar, pregnancy, running. She continues to write on Fiery Pen: The Horror Writing of Christina Bergling and Z0mbie Turtle.

In 2015, she published two novellas. She is also featured in the horror collections *Collected Christmas Horror Shorts*, *Collected Easter Horror Shorts*, *Collected Halloween Horror Shorts*, and *Demonic Wildlife*. Her latest novel, *The Rest Will Come*, was released by Limitless Publishing in August 2017.

Bergling is a mother of two young children and lives with her family in Colorado Springs. She spends her non-writing time running, doing yoga and barre, belly dancing, taking pictures, traveling, and sucking all the marrow out of life.

christinabergling.com

facebook.com/chrstnabergling

@ChrstnaBergling

chrstnaberglingfierypen.wordpress.com

goodreads.com/author/show/11032481.Christina_Bergling

pinterest.com/chrstnabergling

instagram.com/fierypen/

amazon.com/author/christinabergling

Other HellBound Books Titles
Available at: www.hellboundbookspublishing.com

The Waning

Beatrix woke up in a small metal cage, Lost in the darkness, a persistent dripping sound her only company.

She was celebrating a promotion that was the culmination of her entire ruthless, driven career; a promotion that would cement her status enough for her to take her relationship with her girlfriend out of the lesbian closet; Beatrix had finally made it.

And then she was here, disoriented and petrified in a blackness she could not define. Yet the reality of her Master may be even more terrifying than the crushing darkness and enveloping isolation. He appears as an ominous shadow in the doorway of her cell, never speaking. Instead, he teaches Beatrix the language of pain and torture, of submission and obedience, of domination and possession

With each passing day, the fight and hope in Beatrix begins to shrivel and wane. With each savage beating, her survivalist instincts rise up to overwhelm the person she was. With each dehumanizing condition, she begins to forget who she was and the life from which she was ripped.

Can Beatrix ward off the psychological breakdown of her Master? Can she resist the temptation to survive and thrive through submission? Either Beatrix will succeed at surviving and escaping the torments of her Master or her Master will succeed at breaking her completely and reforming her into his design for a human possession…

Dead is Dead, But Not Always

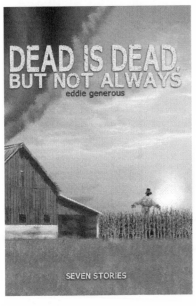

Dead is Dead, but Not Always is the first solo collection from Canadian author Eddie Generous.

The mountain winds Howl and blood flows to appease, tradition runs deep and transforms the skin for the sake of togetherness, buried beneath the soil is a book to bridge the eternal dark with the light of life, God's way is with a hiss but Satan's way is with a kiss, in the Arctic only the bears can hear your screams, when it's your time go the lake will tell you, and being a kid ain't easy when the natural and supernatural collide to peel the layers from your back.

From dread to thriller to cosmic, the seven novelettes collected here meld into one bone-jarringly bleak outing, bound to rattle cores and test readers' nerves.

"The prose is sharp and almost lyrical, the stories not your average fare. These are thoughtful, complex tales that transcend the concept of genre."
—Mark Allan Gunnells, author of Companions in Ruin and The Cult of Ocasta

"Dead is Dead, but Not Always digs into the surreal darkness of your worst nightmares and drags your demons shredding and clawing their way to the treacherous surface of reality."
—Shane Keene, HorrorTalk

<u>Dig Two Graves</u>

In the blurred lines between good and evil - who will win?

Jezebel White is a court-appointed psychologist who runs an underground human trafficking empire.

In order to justify her nefarious actions to her conscience, she selects victims based solely upon whom she deems immoral.

Now, she finds herself being framed for a crime she had only intended to commit.

A detective has placed a target on Jezebel's back, and the time to catch her predator is quickly running out

<u>Sángre: The Color of Dying</u>

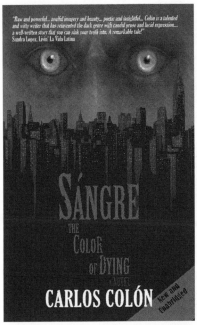

Carlos Colón's first published novel is the story of Nicky Negrón, a Puerto Rican salesman in New York City who is turned into foul-mouthed, urban vampire with a taste for the undesirables of society such as sexual predators, domestic abusers and drug dealers.

A tragic anti-hero, Nicky is haunted by profound loss. When his life is cut short due to an unforeseen event at the Ritz-Carlton, it results in a public sex scandal for his surviving family. He then rises from the dead to become a night stalker with a genetic resistance that enables him to retain his humanity, still valuing his family whilst also struggling to somehow maintain a sense of normalcy.

Simultaneously described as haunting, hilarious, horrifying and heartbreaking, Sángre: The Color of Dying is a breathtakingly fun read.

**A HellBound Books LLC
Publication**

http://www.hellboundbookspublishing.com

Printed in the United States of America